*Love
Letters
on
Leaves*

Arni Phiroz

Copyright © 2020 Arni Phiroz
All rights reserved.

This is a work of fiction. Names, characters and incidents are either the products of the author's imagination or used in a fictitious manner. Any resemblance to actual persons, living or dead, or actual events is purely coincidental.

Cover image: Shutterstock.com

ISBN: 979 8 683755 73 7 (paperback)

For my son
Zal Navroze Phiroz

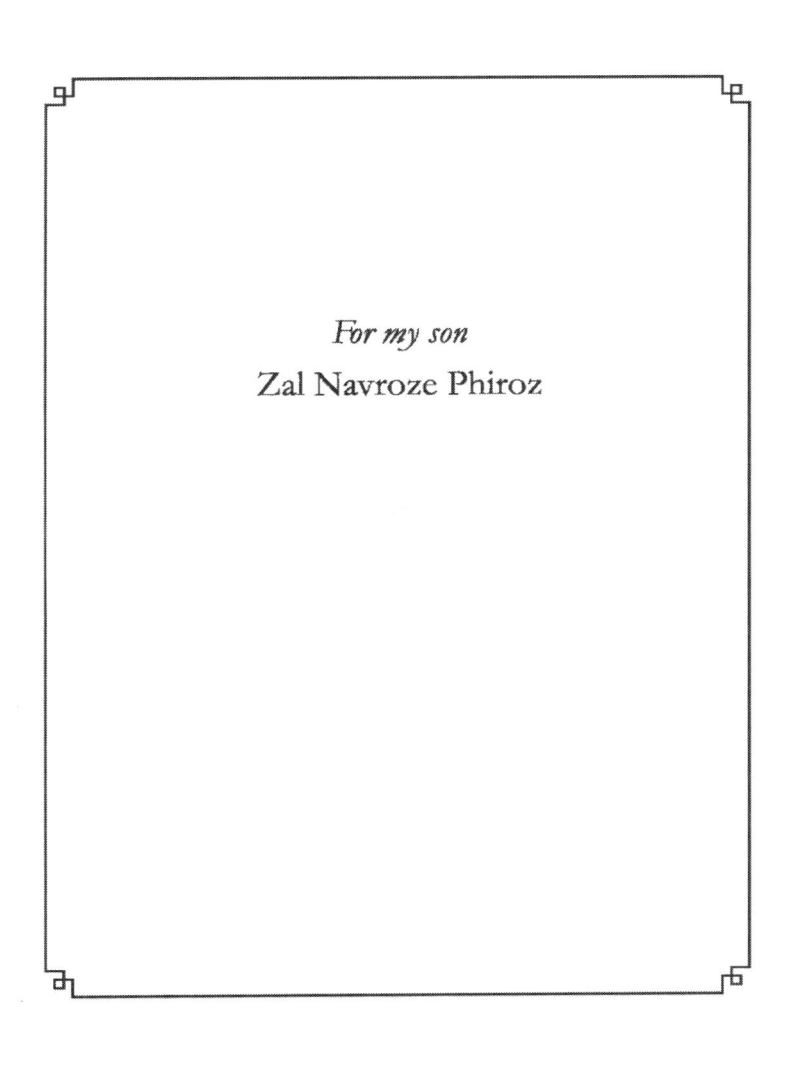

Acknowledgements

I want to acknowledge
Ms. Nawaz Merchant
without whose guidance this book
would not have been possible.

Contents

Chapter 1: A Fleeting Remark 1
Chapter 2: Astrologer 9
Chapter 3: The Cul-de-sac 11
Chapter 4: Accepting 17
Chapter 5: Ava's Arrival 24
Chapter 6: Aunt Jer 27
Chapter 7: Lungri 32
Chapter 8: Jer, Homi and Eruch 35
Chapter 9: The Introduction Charade 40
Chapter 10: The Party 44
Chapter 11: Nergish Lashkari 51
Chapter 12: Adil 55
Chapter 13: Ruby 59
Chapter 14: Ruby Moves In 61
Chapter 15: Ruby the Flight Attendant 64
Chapter 16: Adil's Phone Calls 70
Chapter 17: First Meeting with Adil 73
Chapter 18: Happy Time 79
Chapter 19: Ava's Meeting with her Mother 86
Chapter 20: Adil and Mithu 90
Chapter 21: Love Letters on Leaves 95
Chapter 22: Ava and Adil Meet her Parents 100

Chapter 23: Raju's Training 104

Chapter 24: Ruby's Games 112

Chapter 25: Eruch's Promise 117

Chapter 26: The Attack 119

Chapter 27: The Plan for Ava 123

Chapter 28: Adil in Hospital 129

Chapter 29: Ruby's Getaway 132

Chapter 30: Finding Solutions 138

Chapter 31: Ava's Parents' Decision 146

Chapter 32: Ava Leaves for London 149

Chapter 33: Ava's Arrival in Montreal 152

Chapter 34: Ava's Adjustment 156

Chapter 35: New Experiences 159

Chapter 36: The Persian Garden 168

Chapter 37: A Change of Heart 173

Chapter 38: Snowfall 179

Chapter 39: Valentine's Day 182

Chapter 1
A Fleeting Remark

(Durban, South Africa—1963)

Years later, Ava would remember the day—and the exact moment—her life's trajectory changed. It began with a seemingly inconsequential remark she had made to her doting father. She was feeling burned out after her high school finals, which she had aced.

Stretching and stifling a yawn, she said "Dad, I am not sure I want to study medicine anymore…"

She'd fully expected that her father would understand. After all, it was just the musings of a daughter in need of a brief holiday from her studies.

Her usually indulgent papa would have chuckled and asked, "So where would you like to go this summer? Italy? France?"

She smiled expecting to burst into joyful clapping, when he summoned her mother.

"Dina—come here!" he called out to his wife, who hurried from the kitchen, wiping her hands on her red butcher striped apron.

"Did you hear? Ava doesn't want to go to medical school!" his face flushed with anger.

"If that is her thinking then she must get married!"

Ava could not believe what she was hearing.

She stared at her father. "Dad? Married? I'm only nineteen!" she exclaimed.

But her father wasn't listening. He continued talking to her mother as though it had all been decided.

"Aspi is going to Bombay, the arrangements are all made, and we'll get another ticket on the same flight for Ava."

"This has to be an unusually bad joke dad!" said Ava, with a nervous laugh. But she saw no change of expression from the hard-set lines of his face. With a growing sense of horror, she realized that he was actually serious.

He wanted her married off! And that too within months! Impossible!

Had there been a seismic shift of the earth's plates? What had changed? She tried to mollify her parents.

"Mum, Dad, I didn't mean it. I'm just tired from all these exams."

"Ava," her mother said, "this may be a blessing in disguise, dear. You would have so many exams in medical school. It's sensible to stop now if you don't want to continue studying for another seven plus years."

"But I *do* want to study medicine. *It's all I've ever wanted!*"

Her mother's plump arm encircled her shoulders in a comforting hug.

"She is just exam tired, Darius, give her a little time. I know she has wanted to study medicine since she was knee high!"

"Enough, Dina," her father said with what sounded like a roar, "I have decided."

"It's rather sudden, Darius. Let's give Ava a little more time to reconsider her study path."

To Ava's astonishment, her usually easy-going Dad refused to speak to her.

"I do not want to hear anyone's opinions," he said with unmistakable finality.

"Ava has spoken and so have I. It's final, she will get married at the same time as her brother Aspi. We leave for Bombay next month for both Aspi's and Ava's marriages. End of discussion."

Ava had always wanted to study medicine. She had dreamt of the day she would complete high school and be on a plane to Dublin, Ireland, where her Aunt Khorshed and uncles Edul and Rusi, had qualified as doctors. There was also the ongoing understanding that upon qualifying as a doctor she would take over uncle Edul's practice.

This tornado in her family would pass, Ava told herself. After all, everyone in her family knew how passionately she wanted to study medicine. The knot in her gut cautioned her to heed her father's decision and not regard it as a passing burst of anger.

For the next several weeks, her father's silence and refusal to indulge her in any kind of conversation clearly indicated that she would have to face a huge upheaval in her life, which included dashed hopes of pursuing a career in medicine. To add insult to injury, she was going to be married off in a semi-arranged type of marriage.
The tyranny of old-fashioned tradition, she thought bitterly.

Through her early years in South Africa, Ava had managed to maneuver between her parents' extremely traditional ways and her *au courant* thinking.
Looking back to family dinners over the past years, she realized that she'd been indulged more than most girls. She had been allowed to speak her mind as though she was a son in the family. They'd always encouraged her, and seemed proud of her feisty, modern opinions as she argued against dogmatic traditions.
She knew her parents were more traditional in their approach, since their own semi-arranged marriage was often cited as evidence

that the old ways had proven successful. She had let it pass with a raised eyebrow of wisdom, in knowing when to be quiet. Their old-fashioned thinking had never stood in the way of her happiness... that is, until now. And now it was a disastrous clash of their beliefs versus hers.

With a finger over her mouth, Ava's mother gestured silence to her till her husband's fiery temper had cooled down.

"Ava darling, come sit down, let's talk." She patted the chair next to her at the kitchen table. Ava sat down expecting a lecture about the virtues of ancient traditions and rolled her eyes, sighing as she reluctantly slid into the seat offered to her.

"I can imagine this must have come as a shock to you. But your dad and I have discussed this off and on ever since you morphed into a beautiful young woman. We thought you would always be with us while you were a sickly child for sixteen long years."

"So, I am being punished for overcoming years of eczema and asthma?"

"No, no, sweet one, I am trying to make you understand your dad's stance was not a simple spur of the moment decision."

Dina stroked her daughter's back, trying to find words to soothe her.

"Ava, you know there are no eligible bachelors that you like in our small Parsee community here, right?"

Ava gave a glum nod, not understanding why that had anything to do with her being refused medical school in Dublin.

"Well, sooner or later if you stay here in Durban or go to Dublin, it's likely that you will marry someone that is of another race."

"Yeah, so?" Ava said indignantly.

"Dear child that is not the tradition of this family. You know we pride ourselves on marrying only Parsees."

Ava understood that there were no eligible bachelors in their small Parsee community in the whole of South Africa and her parents' anxiety over her possibly getting involved with someone from a different race.

To Ava that would have been a natural and practical progression. But for her parents, it would be a disgrace to the family.

"But why do I need to go to Bombay of all the places in the world?" asked a still puzzled Ava.

"Bombay is where the largest pool of Parsee bachelor's visits from all over the world to be introduced to their future brides," Dina said.

"Mum is this an arranged marriage proposal or an introduction to a cool Parsee bachelor—if that even exists!" Ava said with disdain, tossing her mane of rich auburn hair sideways.

"Ma, I want to study, study, study, every page of my own Grays Anatomy. I want to *hug* my books. Please talk to Dad and make him change his mind, please mama...." She banged her fists on the table, pleading for her mother's understanding.

Dina nodded and patted Ava's delicate hands.

"I will try my darling child. It's a difficult decision. We both want what is best for your future.

This ridiculous Apartheid system makes it impossible for us to bring a husband to live here in Durban, since as you know, non-whites are not allowed to bring other races into the country, even to visit. It's a dilemma for us and you."

"Is that the crux of the matter, mama? Is that all there is to this crazy idea of me being married off?

The fear that I may marry out of the community?" asked Ava hoping for a way out of this silly conundrum.

Dina was suddenly silent, reticent to say more. Ava was insistent.

"Ma, I know you love me... please tell me why this sudden decision, why now? Why do I feel there is more to this, Ma?"

"Well, there is more to it Ava, my darling child, but..." Dina's affable mood had disappeared and Ava could not nudge her into further conversation.

The next morning, her dad had his head buried in the newspaper. Ava sat silently waiting for him to finish reading so she could speak to him. Finally, he lowered his paper, folded it and put it aside. This was Ava's cue... She looked at him with a tentative smile. Seeing his expression soften, a disarming smile lit up her face. Snuggling up to him as she had done a hundred times before, she hoped to have a cozy chat with him, like they had enjoyed numerous times in the past.

"Daddy, you don't really mean to have me in an arranged marriage, do you?" she said with an engaging smile, as if this were their usual teasing routine.

He avoided her gaze, shifting uncomfortably in his chair.
"Ava, I know this is a strange and sudden turn of events for you. I also understand that living in India can be daunting for a modern young lady like yourself, but I have good reason for wanting this for you," he said calmly. His brow speckled with perspiration and creased in tension betrayed his outer calmness.

"Daddy! How in heaven's name can there be any good reason for trapping me into an arranged marriage in a strange country?" said Ava, in exasperation.
"Ava, I cannot fully divulge my reasons right now. I want you to get married. Later on, you will find that this is the most loving thing I could do for you," he said in a subdued tone.
His perplexing answer further disturbed Ava. Jumping to her feet, she paced back and forth, throwing her hands up in the air, stunned and confused.
"Dad, surely there must be some mistake. How can you think this is the best course of action for my life? This is misery of epic

proportion... all I am asking is to be allowed to study. Please, please, please reconsider, Daddy."

Her father's brows furrowed as he repeatedly rearranged his newspaper.

"Enough, Ava. I don't like tantrums."

"No!" Ava said, swinging around, pushing her face into his line of vision, forcing him to see her. She was frustrated at not being able to get through to her dad, with whom she had rarely exchanged a harsh word.

"You cannot make me go to a new country and marry some stranger. I won't do it and neither you nor the whole world can make me!" Ava turned away from him, her arms folded defiantly across her chest.

She paused to collect her thoughts, then said in a low desperate tone.

"Dad, the only thing that got me through sixteen painful years of illness, all those endless bandages and ointments, eczema and the life-threatening bouts of asthma, was the promise that I would someday go to medical school and qualify as a doctor!"

"You must know that Dad! Surely you must know that! It was the Holy Grail I strived for with every fiber of my being. I know you know that!"

Darius took a deep breath and then spoke again, this time in a slow, controlled manner.

"Ava, I marvel every day at how beautifully you have grown out of your illnesses. You have such fine features, that royal Roman nose that I love," he said, playfully tweaking her nose.

"I also admire your discipline in keeping slim and lithe, but most of all I love the fact that you are so full of love and empathy towards everyone."

There was pain in his voice as he continued, "You are my most valuable asset, Ava. Believe that I have your best interest at heart. Really believe it, because it is true. I understand you need some time to digest this. I know this is an unforeseen development... but I repeat... it is being done in your best interest."

Ava remembered her father, Darius Byramji's, rags to riches story. He never did anything without careful consideration. He was not one to ever give in to a difficult situation... choosing to fight tooth and nail until it was driven to a fair resolution.

The knot in her gut tightened and cautioned her to the fact that her father really seemed to have thoroughly thought through this decision of her marriage.

Feeling like a trapped animal, she struggled, desperate to escape before this unbearable yoke was foisted on her, clearly conscripted into a future that to her was a living nightmare. Even as she strained at the leash, she felt tethered to, there was the realization that life as she had known it, had come to a sudden inglorious end.
It was the perfect storm.

Chapter 2
Astrologer

Durban, South Africa

Mr. Patel, their trusted astrologer, motioned to Ava's anxious mother to take a seat across from him. Dina sat down at the table, noticing it was covered with the same cheap vinyl tablecloth as on her last visit, and patiently waited for him to indicate he was ready.

The astrologer sat down, putting on his old wire-rimmed glasses, which kept slipping to almost the tip of his nose. He opened the latest version of the *Astrologers Almanac*, cleared his throat and finally looked up. This was Dina's cue to speak.

"*Pitaji*[1]*,* my daughter Ava has agreed to accompany the family to Bombay to be introduced to prospective marriage partners."

She paused, hardly believing what she was saying. Then almost breathlessly she continued, "Please *Pitaji*, could you tell me if this is a good time for her marriage?"

She carried on speaking as if unable to stop, "We were hoping that since you have said it was a good time for her brother Aspi to marry, it may be the same for her. We are so keen to see her married into a good family...." Her voice trailed off as she nervously awaited his opinion.

Mr. Patel sighed and thought of the many times over the years that he had heard Dina voice concern regarding her children getting married.

He had however, never known her to say that Ava was agreeable to marriage, let alone one introduced by her family.

---

[1] father

He had known Ava to be caring, intelligent, feisty and headstrong. So, this strong-willed young lady had finally seen this form of matrimony, in a positive light?

More likely, he thought, it was her dad who had broken her fierce spirit, by depriving her of her passion to study medicine.

Interrupting his thoughts, he cleared his throat and concentrated on calculating the position of the stars in Ava's horoscope. He had kept her astrological chart since she was born and the page was yellowing and dog-eared from the many references and readings. He wrote quickly on a pad of lined paper, as he expertly did his mental mathematics. He never used a calculator, preferring to do his complex mathematical calculations the traditional way.

Finally, raising his voice, he spoke, "Ava is coming into a positive time for marriage..."

Dina's face light up and she clasped her hands together and looked up to the heavens as she gave silent thanks to God.

He carried on with concern in his voice, "You must remember this... there will be complications of some type... if you can hurry the marriage through these hurdles, it will be a successful union."

"What type of complications, *Pitaji*?" Dina asked cautiously.

"That I cannot say..." he said, removing his spectacles and shutting his book with finality.

Dina had many questions on her mind, but she knew this was her cue that the reading was over and it was time for her to leave.

"Namaste *Pitaji*, God bless you," she said, clasping her hands together and bowing her head in respect and gratitude. He never accepted money for his services, feeling that his talent would be diminished if he ever did. The only gift he would agree to take was the latest annual version of the *Astrologers Almanac*, which Dina made sure he received every year.

Chapter 3
The Cul-de-sac

Ava paced up and down, peeking out the window every few minutes for a sighting of her mother. She knew that the astrologer's predictions carried a lot of weight with her parents.

His answer could decide if she was going to be sent to India or if it would garner her a reprieve that could instead have her on a plane to Dublin. Catching sight of her mother through the branches of scarlet Flamboyant trees, that lined the hill of Clarence Road, she rushed downstairs.

Dina hurried home, her soft leather sandals swishing over the pavement, her silk saree worn the old-fashioned Parsee way, billowing in the breeze.

Ava had jerked open the front door before her mother had made it up the verandah stairs, and gripped the door handle hard,
as if it would provide courage. She was anxious to hear her fate.

Her mother sat down on the sofa and patted the velvety cushion beside her.
"Ava darling, sit down, sit down, I have wonderful news from *Pitaji*."

Sitting together on the couch, Ava curled into her mother's arms. Dina fondly stroked her cheek and beamed as she spilled out the details of what the astrologer had just told her.
"All is well my darling! It is a good time for you to marry." She hesitated, then said, "He also said something else.
'There will be some complications... you must act quickly and she will have a happy married life... this is the last chance for her happiness... remember not to allow any distractions to delay marriage.'"

Ava's mind whirred, "That's an odd thing to say... Last chance? I'm nineteen for God's sake! What did he mean by complications? What complications, Mum?"

Dina sighed. "He didn't say. But I'll mention this to Daddy, and we'll be ready for whatever lies ahead. *Pitaji* said this is an auspicious time for you to marry, and that's all that matters."

Ava felt a knot in her stomach. Her parents were going ahead with their plans, expecting that she would fall in line. After the furor her refusal had caused, Ava dreaded the next showdown.

Her mother went on, almost talking to herself as she made a list of the many things she had to see to before Ava left for Bombay.
Ava studied her mothers' face, radiant with joy, and felt reluctant to spoil what she knew was an important moment for her.

"Mummy," she said, nervously twisting a strand of her hair, "you know that arranged marriage is archaic Russian roulette and definitely not for me!"
Her mother sighed. "Darling. You have to grow up someday, right? Besides, its only introductions, not arrangements. It's always practiced at every echelon of our society. We would never force you into a marriage, just introduce you to the appropriate bachelors.

I know you love living in Durban, happy under the South African sun... but it's time, sweetheart... time to start a new and exciting chapter of your life."

"Mum, you know what I think of those boys I've met. They bow and scrape to their mothers' wishes with no mind of their own!" she said with disgust.

Ava scoffed. She had laughed off the few local eligible Parsee bachelors that came asking for her hand in marriage, disdainfully regarding them as "Mama's boys."

"Well Ava, as you know the few local Parsee boys are not to your liking, so have courage, and we will find you a suitable partner in Bombay where there are plenty of young Parsee bachelors" her mother replied with optimism.

Dina had experienced a similar scenario with her own parents so she understood Ava's dilemma. She sat at the foot of Ava's bed, speaking to her in a soothing voice. Ava buried her head in her hands, thinking that this was certainly looking like a no-win situation for her.

South Africa was the only country in the world to openly practice Apartheid, a word which in Afrikaans meant 'Separateness.' The Afrikaners who were in political power carried out a comprehensive brutality in segregating the entire country based solely on the color of your skin. People of India or any Asian country were classified as Non-white and treated with utter contempt by the government.

Every facet of a person's life was defined by the color of their skin from the day of birth to death. Everyday privileges were decided on one's race and ethnicity. Ava and her family were classified "Non-white" and forced to live within the boundaries of Apartheid.

The Group Areas Act meant Ava's family could only live in certain areas of the city designated for their race category, and could forcibly be evicted from their homes by the government by simply rezoning the area for "Whites-only," on the turn of a dime.

This had happened to the family several times since Ava was born. Ava accepted the numerous boundaries that came with this classification.

The Immorality Act was clear. Non-Whites could not associate with Whites. There was zero tolerance of any such interactions and infringement resulted in imprisonment. All entertainment, hotels and restaurants were segregated. Department stores enforced a ban on Non-Whites trying on clothing before buying and to add insult to injury, they were not able to change the size or return it, once bought.

Even the white-sandy beaches that glistened like sugar, had large boards declaring "Whites only." The beaches that Non-Whites were allowed on had jagged rocks and dangerous undercurrents.

Ava accepted it all, the constant moving of homes; the cold, rude reception from the sales-ladies when she shopped for clothes and shoes, never being allowed to try on clothes before buying and no exchanges allowed; the total exclusion of staying at a hotel of choice or being served at a restaurant; even the debris that hurt her feet when she stepped on the sand at the beach. She had become accustomed to it.

The only part of Apartheid that totally frustrated Ava was that all universities were for "Whites-only," with no exceptions... and therefore, they were shut off to her.

From a young age, Ava had her future all planned out. After high school she would go to Dublin, Ireland, and study Medicine. This had been her passion through all the years her strong spirit had fought her frail health. While qualifying as a doctor, she would likely meet and marry a fellow colleague. All her aunts and uncles had studied medicine in Dublin at the Royal College of Surgeons and that is where they had met their life partners; she was going to follow in their footsteps. She felt passionate about everything to do with health and medicine.

The year after high school that she had hoped to spend as her first year at university, ended up being spent in restless fits of shopping because of her refusal to go to Bombay and get married coupled with the Apartheid setup at the local universities.

Most young ladies would have envied her wardrobe of exquisite dresses, shoes, handbags, custom-made jewelry and anything else she fancied in the stores. But all she wished for is being able to exchange it all for medical textbooks and university courses.

Her parents expected a strict code of obedience to their wishes. Important life decisions were made by them and Ava was expected to follow them. Of profound importance to them was marriage to someone that fit their list of "must haves;" wealth, social standing and an irreproachable reputation were their criteria for the man who married their daughter. Any whiff of scandal or social faux pas either on Ava's part or her suitors would render them ineligible for marriage and would be met with shock and outrage.
All her life, Ava had practiced restrained discipline and obedience, never showing her true feelings freely to anyone other than persons her parents deemed socially acceptable.

She was coming to the realization that her only options were either to co-operate with her parents and agree to marry someone they approved of or endlessly fritter her life away with idle frivolities.

Alone in her room, even with the door shut she could hear the joy in her mother's voice as she conveyed *Pitaji's* astrological reading to her dad, over the phone. She slumped to the floor next to her bed, crumpling her soft white silk dress. Sobs came from deep inside her, painfully, mercifully releasing some of the pain at the loss of her dreams, her passions, her now never-to- be-fulfilled need to study medicine. She would never be able to hug her copy of *Gray's Anatomy*; research for cures of diseases would have to be done by someone else. Working with Doctors without Borders, or free clinics for people who needed medical skill, knowledge and compassion were out of her reach.

She had followed rules all her life, so why was it so difficult to obey this one? She felt like she was exchanging the shackles of her long illness and Apartheid for another type of sentence... Marriage.

Her beloved Durban had become a cul-de-sac.

Chapter 4
Accepting

Ava thought of the million little things that had made her love her life in Durban. The white-washed double-storeyed mansion high up on Clarence Road Hill beside neighboring mansions and lifestyles awash with wealth and gaiety.

Their three-tiered terraced garden was landscaped with luxuriant Birds of Paradise, their majestic heads of gold and blue, standing upright like proud soldiers. Alongside were a myriad variety of dahlias in rust brown, blood red, bright yellow, deep ochre with floors of gold-flecked purple pansies, peaceful white lilies and daisies in oranges and pinks, waving cheerily in the breeze.
She would always want to live here!

The sunshiny days, cool evening breezes, the playful abandonment at the beach, the idyllic and indulgent lifestyle her parents she had enjoyed…. She walked through the garden admiring the jacaranda and flamboyant trees that lay a luxurious carpet of purple and red flowers. The sweet peas with their tendrils climbing up the wire trellis were like a watercolor painting.
Sitting on the immaculately trimmed lawn, she felt the cool, comforting grass under her fingers. To add to her continued pleasure were her pets, Chili the parrot, who got his name because he loved eating red chilies and her silky, playful, golden retriever puppy, Rolo.

Then there was the volunteering at the Freedom Clinic, where she got to make patients comfortable and watch them heal. Oh God, how she loved it! Life was wonderful, she thought with a wistful sigh.

She walked through the garden marveling at the forty-year- old avocado tree that gave them an abundance of fruit to share with all their friends and still kept on giving. From the backyard she heard the thud of another avocado falling to the ground without being plucked. The huge avocado tree supplying large baskets of the creamy rich fruit. She would miss her avocado on toast with a sprinkle of salt and freshly ground pepper that was her usual mid-afternoon snack. Sometimes she would indulge the family in the way they liked to eat their avocados, mashed and mixed with honey.

Yum! one of the best desserts she had tasted.

The gardener had mowed the lawns and left a small pile of freshly cut grass in the corner of the garden. Ava remembered how she loved walking into the pile of grass that he always remembered to leave for her. She would close her eyes relishing the fresh greenness under her feet.

The climbing profusion of fuchsia bougainvillea had looped itself over the immaculately trimmed fence that bordered the huge garden and partially hid the ugly but necessary electric fencing and security cameras.

Ava was shocked out of her reverie by a soul-curdling scream she recognized as likely being that of one of their maids. An angry voice with a strong Afrikaner accent shouted, "Where is your Pass Book!"

Startled, Ava ran toward the ruckus, remembering that Blacks were obligated to carry a Pass Book which held all their personal details.

"It's at home!" the maid said, her voice trembling.

"You know you should always have it on your person, you stupid Kaffir!" came the loud, high-pitched Afrikaner accent.

"Oh, sorry, sorry Big Baas!" the maid pleaded.

The next thing Ava heard was the sickening thuds of the butt- end of a *knobkerrie*[2] smashing repeatedly at the maid.

The young servant cried out, "No, please Baas, I have it, I have it," to no avail. She was steps away from her Pass Book which lay in the outhouse, at the back of the mansion. But Ava knew that the aim of the Afrikaner police officer was not to show any fairness to a Black person, but rather to deliver as harsh a punishment as possible, with the intent of breaking their spirit.

She heard the scuffle amid shrieks of pain from the maid being pushed into the police van and the doors being slammed shut. She knew any interference could have no positive outcome and would likely result in her being carted away in the same horrible fashion as the maid.

The bubble of her halcyonic lifestyle had burst, underlining the dangers lurking outside the carefully guarded boundaries of her home.

She stumbled to the bathroom and over the sink gave herself up to waves of retching and the rude reality of her living in South Africa.

Mopping her face with a cool facecloth, she remembered her dad saying," I love you Ava, and believe me when I say, I am choosing this option with your best interest at heart."

He had never let her down, always loved her, so she was going to put her hand in his and hope to God she could summon the inner strength to comply with his wishes.

She had run out of choices. Her beloved Durban had become a cul-de-sac and the only way out was to acquiesce to her parents' wishes.

When she came to the kitchen that evening, her mother looked surprised. Noticing Ava's reddened features, she winced. "Oh, my beautiful daughter... have you been crying again?"

---

[2] a stout wooden cane with a large wooden knob at one end

"No." Ava said resignedly. "I'll do it. I'll go to Bombay and try it your and Dad's way."

"Oh! That's wonderful news!" Dina cried, smiling. "How unexpected! How marvelous! My headstrong daughter, you've surprised us again. Your papa will be so glad."

It was time to be practical, Ava told herself. She had been stubborn about wanting to lead her life, her way. But it was a losing battle. Durban, South Africa in the 1960s offered no part-time jobs for "Non-whites." Every young person was totally dependent on their parents or guardians for their welfare and all expenses. There was no such thing as standing on your own two feet or roughing it and staying on your own. It just was not possible in that part of the world. She was firmly under her parents' control and fighting and railing against it with all her might would have no effect.

Shaking herself out of her low spirits she resolved to think and act positively.

First, she made a list of all the things she needed to do to get ready for her new role as an aspiring bride-to-be. Next, she started thinking about the wardrobe she would take with her. This would be different from any of her other trips. She did not know how long she would be gone or if she would ever return to her beloved Durban. She firmly pushed aside the thought that she may never return. Of course, she was just being silly, she thought. Now she concentrated on that most important of matters... her trousseau and the extensive, perfectly planned, wardrobe of clothes and accessories she would need.

Shopping, glorious shopping, bags and bags of marvelous clothes and shoes wrapped in multicolored tissue. She rolled back on her bed, laughing and suddenly excited at the prospect of preparing herself for something daunting, but very possibly fun.

She picked up the phone and dialed the phone number of her best friend, Kay. She and Kay had been inseparable girlfriends for many years and had enjoyed a rollercoaster ride of adventures of all kinds. They could find the funny side of any situation.

"Hello, Kay?" she said, smiling in anticipation of being with her friend.

"Kay, how do you feel about shopping till we drop?" "Sure," replied Kay, laughing out aloud.

"Listen, I have decided to go along with the marriage introduction proposition..."

There was a long silence. "Kay, are you there?"

She was answered by a gasp of surprise from her friend, "Ava, are you seriously considering this?" she asked.

"Yes, I am. In fact, I have already agreed to go along with my parents' plans," she replied in a barely audible whisper.

"So, the all-important shopping begins today?" Kay asked.

"Yes, shall we meet at my place for a late breakfast and then we can walk into town?" Ava suggested.

"Shopping... is there anything more fun in this world!" Kay said with her usual high spirits.

After Ava hung up, it dawned on her that they had not agreed on what time Kay would be over. She guessed it would likely be 11am. After generous helpings of delicious French toast and steaming cups of black Darjeeling tea, flavored with lemon grass and mint, they would walk the short distance into town and browse the imaginatively decorated windows of the large, busy, department stores.

After she spoke to Kay her impulse was to duck under the covers and hope it would all go away. But instead, she summoned her disciplined self to action. Slipping into her silk slippers, she realized it was already past nine o'clock. She quickly brushed her teeth, showered and got herself ready for her foray into the marvelous world of fashion and retail therapy.

Putting on her apron, she slipped into her sanctuary, the kitchen. When life got complex, she would lose herself creating something delicious for her family and friends. With her jittery nerves this morning, she decided on making French toast the way she and Kay loved it.

Cracking eggs in a bowl, she whisked in some maple syrup which her cousin had sent from Canada, put in pinches of nutmeg and cinnamon and a generous spoonful of vanilla. She dipped the thick slices of the raisin bread that she had baked a few days ago, into the egg mixture and slipped them into a hot pan sizzling with butter.

The doorbell rang just as the kettle started whistling and the last of the French toast in the pan had been turned over.

Kay was at the door. They hugged as they walked into the hallway. The fragrance of nutmeg, cinnamon, maple syrup and butter filled the sunny kitchen and lifted her spirits.

Kay, familiar with the kitchen, helped make the tea, deftly combining the dark Darjeeling with a dash of Earl Grey and set it on the large table that had already been laid with a cheery yellow- checked tablecloth, napkins, plates and heavy silver cutlery. Ava placed a platter of golden French toast and a jug of maple syrup on the table and they both sat down.

They paused looking at each other intently for a long moment, both realizing that these carefree breakfasts they had shared so many times in the past, may well be one of their last.

Determined to inject some lightness into the somber moment, Ava concentrated on pouring the steaming tea into their cups, forked slices of French toast onto Kay's plate and started discussing suggestions for the all-important new wardrobe of clothes and accessories.

Soon the mood turned light-hearted and their conversation was filled with the giddy excitement of shopping for a trousseau and other feminine accessories that Ava would need for the many events she would be attending in Bombay. They had shopped together for years but this was going to be different. Every piece of clothing had to be meticulously coordinated and appropriately accessorized. It would likely be their last shopping spree together

Chapter 5
Ava's Arrival

A month later, as the plane touched down at Bombay airport, Ava tried to face her second visit to Bombay with a positive attitude. She was travelling alone and planned to meet up with her parents and Aspi, her elder brother, all of whom had gone to Bombay earlier, to prepare for his upcoming nuptials.

Entering the airport, which at 2 am was still extremely busy, she looked up disdainfully at the ceiling fans whirring in vain, trying to cool the oppressively hot air. She got into the long Customs and Immigration queue. She had been here before and felt familiar with the way things worked. When her turn came, she handed over her passport, and declared the many pieces of valuable jewelry she was carrying. The jewelry was intended to be worn at her brother's upcoming wedding in Bombay.

The large amount of bank drafts and jewelry that was stamped on her passport caused the Customs Officer to probe her reason for bringing in the jewels and money.
"What do you need these jewels for?" he asked raising his eyebrows.
"They are to be worn at my brother's upcoming wedding," she replied truthfully.
The customs officer was accustomed to distrust responses to his questions.
"People always lie," he thought. His red paan-stained teeth showed, as he unabashedly leered at her breasts. She averted her eyes and said nothing, aware that those bank drafts stamped on her passport would have to be accounted for before she left India. Indian law firmly stated that the drafts had to be cashed at the Bank of India.

She was well aware that her father was not going to do that and instead planned to sell it for more than its face value on the black market.

What she did not realize then, is the crucial part they would play in deciding her fate.

Finally, she was out of the stifling heat of the airport and into the fresh, early morning air. Hailing a taxi, she settled back for the long drive to Gowalia Tank and her Aunt Jer's spacious apartment.

The taxi passed the Hanging Gardens. The cool, morning breeze, heavy with the fragrance of jasmine and roses, eased her trepidation at this dreaded visit. Closing her eyes, she took deep breaths of this beautiful part of Bombay. It brought to mind the colorful and intoxicatingly fragrant *gajra*[3] and her longing to wear one in her hair.

Jeweled tiaras could not hold a candle to the beauty of the *gajra*, she thought. The *gajra* and its captivating scent enhanced the beauty of every woman that wore one in her hair.

She smiled at the thought of her sweet-natured Aunt Jer, and the apartment which spanned half of the entire floor of the 4-storey building. The numerous windows which overlooked the Gowalia Tank *maidan*[4] were also an open window into the daily lives of the pavement dwellers below. The park was mainly a dusty, barren area, without much greenery or anything that resembled a park. It did, however, have a precious commodity that sustained the pavement dwellers, a tap with running water. That water fed families who lived on the small stretch of pavement across the building and along the iron fence bordering the open *maidan*.

The taxi driver was speaking to her, "*Memsahib, Memsahib*, 100 rupees."

---

[3] garland of jasmine and other scented flowers
[4] field or park

The familiar smells of horse and cow dung mixed with various types of pollution made her realize they had arrived at Gowalia Tank.

For a moment she took stock of her surroundings. The swarm of humanity, traffic and animals took up every inch of the road. One could barely see the pavement or street. There were rickshaws bicycling people to their destination, a crush of taxis incessantly honking, impatient drivers, flagrantly disregarding any driving rules, and pedestrians jostling each other to get to wherever they needed to go.

Anyone slowing down the pace would likely be pushed over and possibly stepped on.

Adding to the congestion, were oxen- pulled carts and cows walking leisurely across the road. The latter brought all traffic to a screeching halt. No one dared hurry the errant cow. Wandering cows causing giant traffic jams was unquestioned. The cow was revered and no one dared show any disrespect to this animal. Nothing much had changed, she thought.

Paying the driver, she gingerly stepped onto the pavement at the entrance to the building. Having to avoid stepping into something rotting or filthy was a skill one developed after having lived there for some time. Thank goodness, the monsoons were not here to ruin her numerous pairs of dainty sandals.

On her last visit the monsoons were in full force. She shuddered as she remembered... she had barely taken two steps from the building entrance into a waiting taxi, when a large rat, the size of a fully-grown cat, emerged from a flooded gutter and slapped against her leg. Her aunt had quickly pushed her into the taxi, before she fainted in shock.

To Aunt Jer, it was all part of the territory one had to skillfully navigate, if you wanted to live in Bombay.

Chapter 6
Aunt Jer

Rats, pollution, dust, beggars, jostling through swarms of people—these things did not daunt Aunt Jer, thought Ava with a smile. Her aunt was indomitable in most ways of Bombay life. Always well-dressed, energetic and sociable, she lived a privileged lifestyle. Being childless, she doted on Ava.

Her aunt seemed to throw herself into the local social scene with enthusiasm. She and Uncle Homi were invited to just about every lavish Bombay wedding, and had numerous affluent friends. They in turn, hosted spectacular soirées with a variety of fun themes. Jer lived for parties, and was usually the life of the party herself. No wonder, Ava thought, such get-togethers assured them their place within the social elite of Bombay. Within a few short weeks, Ava found herself a part of this whirlwind of fun-filled, seemingly endless parties.

Jer's daily activities had an almost humorous pattern to them. It began when the door-bell rang at around 7am, and Aunt Jer ran, sandals clickety-clacking on the marble floor to open it. The first of two servants arrived. The first servant entered, saree covering her face, ready to clean only the toilets, as she was from the Untouchable Hindu caste. She'd go from home to home each day, silently cleaning only toilets. She came and went like a ghost with no acknowledgement of her work or word of thanks. Housewives paid her a pittance each week, dropping the coins into her palm in silence.

Ava shuddered thinking of the poor woman's life. How awful to have to wake up every morning and go house to house cleaning people's filthy toilets. But since she was from the Untouchable caste, that was the only work that was available to her.

By the time the first vendor rang the doorbell, Aunt Jer was dressed in a fresh cotton saree. After that, the doorbell rang almost every hour or two. Jer would run to peer through the door slats, inquire who was there, even though she could clearly see who it was.

The vegetable seller arrived and rang the bell, lowering his basket of fresh vegetables from the top of his head and placing it on the ground. He wiped his hot, sweaty face with the cloth he wore on his head as a cushion for the heavy basket. He was perspiring heavily after having to climb two flights of stairs.

"Yes, what is it?" asked Aunt Jer looking at what he had to offer and feigning disinterest.

"*Memsahib*, I have brought you fresh vegetables!" he said, wiping his brow again.

Jer shut the door and speaking to him through the door slats said, "I don't see anything that interests me, come back tomorrow if you have some really fresh vegetables!"

The tall, thin man, dressed in a worn-out cotton lungi and shirt rattled off the merits of his produce.

Jer opened the door and still showing disinterest in his produce, proceeded to bargain with him for the few items that she found acceptable. The door was again slammed shut for a few minutes.

Through the door slats Jer inquired in a take it or leave it tone, "What price do you want for the vegetables?"

The poor, anxious vendor rattled of the prices, begging her to buy his produce at a very nominal price, which he said he had reduced, just for her. Jer opened the door, took the vegetables and paid him the small sum in coins.

"Thank you, *Memsahib*, thank you," he said bowing. "I will bring you more fresh produce tomorrow." With that transaction complete, he sighed deeply and once again placed the rolled cloth on his head and placed his basket on it.

Jer shut the door, pleased with her bargaining prowess. This game or manner of purchasing, repeated itself with the fish vendor, the fruit vendor and all the vendors, who brought their wares to the door.

The only one exempt from the bargaining was the milk man. His price was always the same. She silently offered her vessel to be filled and he ladled the milk into it, collected his money and left.

How curious, thought Ava. Aunt Jer ran to every ringing doorbell, and never tired of the daily bargaining. The poor wretches had no alternative, she thought. If they did not cooperate, Aunt Jer would buy from someone who did.

Feeling humiliated for the vendors, Ava asked, "Aunt Jer, why don't you pay these poor people the price they ask for?"

Jer retorted with exasperation, "Ava, they would not respect me if I paid them what they wanted... absolutely out of the question!"

She felt put-out by Ava's remark, and went on, "They deliberately inflate their prices and only bargaining with them results in fair prices. Ava don't be swayed by the gaunt and haggard appearance of the vendors; they all look like that!"

Her air of finality made Ava shake her head in disbelief. What surprised Ava was that the same vendors returned daily and the same bargaining, purchasing ritual was repeated. To Ava who had never experienced this type of daily bargaining act, it was simultaneously bewildering and hilarious, a tragicomedy played out for the same audience every day.

The last doorbell ring usually marked the arrival of the second servant, who cleaned the rest of the home. She spent several hours sweeping and swabbing the tiled floors, carrying out her duties with her saree covering most of her face and in invisible silence. Before she left for the day, her last task was to fill the large clay urns in each room with fresh drinking water. She left, bowing with a silent Namaste to Aunt Jer and Ava.

Ava felt she was witnessing discrimination here again in Bombay, with the servants being treated with the same indignity as the Non-whites and black Africans in South Africa. In India, Apartheid took the form of the caste system in determining the limitations of one's lifestyle. In South Africa, the Apartheid criteria was the color of one's skin.

From Aunt Jer's spacious apartment on the entire second floor, Ava had a bird's eye view of the pavement dwellers who resided along the park fence directly across from Aunt Jer's building and could observe the amazingly normal manner in which they conducted life's daily rituals.

"Aunt Jer, do you know the pavement dwellers living across the road?"

Her aunt scowled, looking at her without lifting her head. "Why do you want to know Ava?" icicles could have formed in her tone.

Ava was going to say she would have liked to get to know them but observing her aunt's displeasure decided instead to ask if she knew their names.

"Yes, Ava, the one-legged lady is simply called Lungri(cripple) and her son is Raju. Next to her lives Rani, her husband, three sons and one daughter named Devi. Neighboring them is a single mother named Sita with a baby named Mithu.

Now listen to me please when I say that you are not to speak to them or give them money. Do you understand, Ava?"

Ava did not understand why but noting Aunt Jer's stern demeanor she looked down and nodded.

Witnessing the relentlessly hard life of the pavement dwellers, Ava was fascinated by their easy-going acceptance of their lot in life and camaraderie. They were all hopelessly poor, with the ladies doing menial work to support their families. Yet she saw them sharing their meagre rations of food and in emergencies, money as well.

Her own problems seemed infinitesimal compared to theirs.

Chapter 7
Lungri

It was a clammy humid Sunday evening when Ava heard someone shouting loudly from the street. One-legged *Lungri*[5], ran, expertly balancing herself on one crutch. She pointed and yelled at the tramp who had slumped on the portion of the pavement that was her 'home.'

Her eyes blazing with anger, she poked the man with her crutch, shouting obscenities and warnings. No filthy squatter was going to take her home, which was a small portion of the pavement that backed onto the park in Gowalia Tank.

Lungri had just returned from her various jobs, each day blurring into the next in a never-ending sequence of hot sun and trudging from one building to another. Her weeks rarely differed.

At dawn she got up off her mat, taking her six-year-old son to the cold-water tap in the park. Here she would wash him and herself, fill a pot with water and return to her mat on the pavement.

Pulling out her precious box of belongings that consisted of a pot, a flat *chapati*[6] pan, a large cooking spoon, two cups, one *thali*[7], flour, oil, tea, sugar, spices and a few clothes, she would light the Primus stove and boil water for their sugared tea breakfast, wash the tin cups at the tap, and carefully and quickly drape a clean saree around herself, leaving her son to wear his precious school clothes. Then, oiling her son's hair and combing it, she set him down with his slate and chalk, while she deftly coiled her hair into a neat bun, and tended to her own basic makeup, applying black *kajal*[8] and a red *bindi*[9] to her forehead, to remind the world she was a married woman and not a slut.

---

[5] a lame person
[6] flatbread
[7] tray
[8] eyeliner

She rolled up the mat and put it away beside the box, next to the iron park fence, hobbling a little while, she got control of her crutch. Accompanying her son to the school gate, she hurried to her first of several daily cleaning jobs.

Lungri had been born an "Untouchable," so the only type of work she was permitted to do was clean toilets. Her day was spent going from home to home, cleaning toilets. She did not mind her tasks, having accepted since she was very young that it was the only way to earn a living. The lazy father of her son, Raju, had disappeared a long time ago. She was proud of the fact that she could support herself and Raju, and sometimes have a little extra money to take him to the movies.

That evening she'd saved enough to take him to see the latest Indian movie. What a treat! It had been months since she had a few rupees to spare. The movie would once again sweep them away into a world of dancing and clandestine romance with happy endings.

Emerging into the quiet night air from the theatre, elated, they would walk hand in hand, with happy smiles, to their sliver of a pavement home. Raju talked non-stop, his high-pitched little voice eagerly reliving the fight-scene, the chase, and the horseback riding. She smiled indulgently, happy to have given him something to get excited about.

Unrolling their mat onto their portion of the filthy pavement, she covered them both with a blanket, watching her son who was still spellbound by the movie.

Arms softly wrapped around Raju, her dreams overtook her. Someday Raju and she would also live in a huge mansion like the one in the movies. She would be the *Memsahib*, dressed in brightly colored silk and jewelry, ordering servants to bring her tea and sweets. The servants would bow and address her as *Memsahib*, lady of the home.

---

[9] dot on the forehead

"Yes, Raju and I will be safe," she dreamt. She'd named her son Raju, which meant King. "Someday soon he will live like a king."

In the darkness the hope did not seem so foolish. For now, she was content to sleep under the stars, on a hard pavement, with a thin mat under her, shielded from the elements by a flimsy blanket.

How could Lungri have guessed that her humble life struggles were having a profound effect on Ava?

Chapter 8
Jer, Homi and Eruch

The highlight of Eruch's life was being an Income Tax Officer. The power he had over people gave him an air of invincibility.

A short, pale, skinny man with a pencil thin moustache, he had never married and lived with his spinster sister in a small apartment. No one was ever invited to his apartment and most of his friends did not even know he had a sister or anything about his family.

His attire of white pants and white shirt with well-worn suede shoes, never changed, regardless of the many social events he attended. No one would dare mention it. Everyone who knew him was eager to be in his good books. After all, one never knew when they might need a favor from him. Eruch was well aware of this and never played down his sense of importance.

Jer and Homi (Jer's husband) had endured a long, hastily put together arranged marriage by their parents, decades ago. They could not be more incompatible if they had tried. But they made their marriage work by throwing themselves into the gay socialite world where life's realities were never closely examined.

They had invited Eruch to stop over for drinks, before they left for the Annual Gala Dinner at the Taj Hotel. Homi resplendent in his black silk custom-tailored suit and patent ballroom dance shoes, smiled at his reflection in the hallway mirror, before ushering Eruch in. Pouring them both Scotch and sodas, they exchanged the latest political *faux pas* in the news.

Recognizing the familiar sound of Jer's heels clicking along the marble hallway, they both stood as she entered the living room.

Wearing a cool turquoise chiffon saree, richly beaded with pearls and sequins, designed and embroidered to her specifications, she entered looking poised, elegant and cheerful.

"Gentlemen, shall we go?" she asked smiling.

Homi and Eruch nodded, emptying their glasses with one last gulp.

"I think it's going to be a spectacular evening!" she said excitedly, as she gave herself the once over in the hallway mirror. She had been right about choosing the flawless blue and white diamond and pearl earrings, necklace and bracelet, as it beautifully complimented her saree. The earrings alone had diamonds that were in excess of 5 carats. They felt heavy and regal and she loved the way they caught the light at every angle.

"Eruch, you are staring!" exclaimed Jer, giving him a questioning look and a gentle nudge with her shoulder.

"Jer, I well uh... I have never seen anything so magnificent!" he said, unable to take his eyes off the glitter of Jer's jewelry.

"Eruch, I wish you meant I was the magnificent one!" she chided. "But I can see you are taken by my choice of jewelry." She said turning her head sideways and touching her earlobes.

"These jewels were an inheritance from my mother, Shirinbai, who personally chose each gem used in every piece she designed. Since the jewels were extremely valuable, Shirinbai would insist the jeweler stay in her home, while he turned her designs into the magnificent heirlooms they would become." Jer smiled at the thought of her incredibly talented mother.

"Your mother came all the way from South Africa to India?" Eruch inquired incredulously.

"Yes... every year, she would make the long journey from Durban to Bombay by ship, bringing with her sketches of her designs together with the gems, to be turned into spectacular pieces of jewelry.

After reaching Bombay and visiting her many relatives each of whom received a generous envelope of money, she would summon her jeweler and settle in to oversee him turning the gems and gold into breathtaking pieces of art. It was understood that he would stay in her home for as many days or weeks necessary to complete all her designs." She sighed and nodded, nostalgically recalling those magical times.

Arriving at the majestic entrance of the Taj Hotel, Jer thanked the smartly liveried chauffeur, without looking at him directly. Stepping onto the red carpet at the entrance, she adjusted the folds of her saree that had briefly shifted during the drive to the Taj. Turning to gaze briefly at the full moon shimmering over the dark Arabian Sea, across from the Taj, she shrugged off the vague, passing thought, that the chauffeur would likely park Eruch's old Ambassador car around the corner, light a *beedi*[10], and settle in for a long wait before he could go home to his wife and children asleep in their tin-and-plastic-sheeting shack.

Homi patiently waited, encouraging Jer to take his arm which she did with a skip in her step. The sound of music and revelry coming from the ballroom quickened her excitement and she tugged at Homi's arm ready to dance as the drums sounded a crescendo and a new artist took the stage. There was pleasure to be had, and Jer was ready to let it lift her up and swirl around her. She was in her element here among her glitterati friends as she smiled and waved and blew air kisses to the many familiar faces that recognized her.

---

[10] hand-rolled cigarette

Eruch stroked his thin moustache and smiled expectantly as he saw Ruby. His excitement heightened as he approached her. Joining Ruby at the buffet table, he kissed her on the cheek, showering her with compliments on her appearance. She gave him a flirty, knowing look, her eyelashes brushing her cheek.

The gala had just begun, an hour earlier and the orchestra members sported brows lightly beaded with perspiration. They were into a spirited version of "I'm in Heaven" as Homi in his shiny dancing shoes, expertly whirled Jer around the dance floor. She gave Eruch a friendly wave as she caught sight of him

. Eruch was already giddy with anticipation at the possible pleasures the titian-haired Ruby may make possible for him that evening.

He looked around to see who had escorted her to the Gala.

His eyes would be following their moves throughout the evening, while he wandered around the room, exchanging shallow pleasantries with the many beautiful people there.

Eruch was too finicky to participate in any sexual acts himself, preferring instead to peep through a window or a slightly open door, while Ruby moaned and gyrated in orgasmic ecstasy. The sight of her having sex with other men, caused him to be sexually aroused and giggle uncontrollably.

Ruby knew Eruch's fetishes and her power over him. She always maintained an air of promising seduction and forbidden pleasures to come. She may need a favor from Eruch someday, she thought, as she smiled at him, inviting him into her world of promiscuity and thrills.

He walked over to Jer and Homi and mentioned that his chauffeur would take them home whenever they were ready. He would be staying a lot longer, winking at them which was a signal that he expected an especially good time watching Ruby and her new escort.

Ruby was such a clever little minx, he thought. How had she managed to get away from her fiancé, Adil, he wondered.

Chapter 9
The Introduction Charade

The days that followed Eruch's party were a blur of meetings with marriage matchmakers, interested families and their sons. Ava dutifully attended all the soirées and introductions, impeccably dressed, coifed and mannered, losing count of the numerous handshakes and pleasantries. She politely endured being looked over by prospective young men, their mothers and aunts, as though she were merchandise displayed in a store.

"Dina, I must compliment you on your daughter's exquisite figure. Her complexion is flawless, perhaps a tad too tanned for our sons. You must be very proud of her." They unanimously commented.

"Dear, what do you mean by "too tanned?" asked Dina, completely flummoxed by the similarity of the comments she was hearing.

"Well, Dina. The thing is…we were hoping for a girl with a fairer complexion!"

So, the consensus was that the fairer and whiter the skin, the better. Basically, they were following the British colonial standard of beauty. "Apartheid in Bombay," thought Ava. It didn't matter what qualities she possessed or what her opinions were—the fewer she had of those the better!

White skin was all that mattered in Apartheid South Africa, and here in Bombay, India, she was seeing similar discrimination…from her own community. She had agreed to this preposterous agreement for the love of her parents and the limitations South Africa had offered but she hated this whole charade, piqued at the shallowness of the reception she was receiving.

"Why, it's more like a lampooning than an introduction!" she thought, her irritation growing with each passing day.

Her Dad had always called her his 'Spanish princess,' because of her long swan-like neck, and golden complexion. The whole process of mothers deciding which young lady made the best match for their immature sons was a flawed crapshoot, Ava thought in frustration.

She knew her parents cared deeply for her. Being married into a family of their social status, she was repeatedly told, would secure her a lifetime of happiness. The other important factor she had to remember was that the family's esteemed reputation must be upheld, since that too was the duty of a good daughter.

Jer took one look at Ava's face as she returned from her umpteenth matchmaking session and said, "You need baking therapy!"
Amused, Ava washed her hands, wishing she could flush the whole introduction process down the drain.
"Aunt Jer, how many of these milksops must I meet before one decent young man is introduced to me?" she said rolling her eyes.
"Can you imagine, the family I met today had the surname of Sodabottleopenerwalla. How on earth can I go around with a surname like that!" she exclaimed with exasperation.

"I understand dear," Jer said after recovering from a fit of laughter. "I know it can be a difficult process... But I must say the way you express it is a breath of fresh air!"

"Ava dear," Jer went on, "you must be practical. My marriage to Homi was a quickly arranged affair. You know my father had a jewelry business. Our wedding was planned to neatly fit into our parents' business schedules."

"It sounds so... cold," Ava said softly.

Jer shook her head. "To our fathers it may have been an obligation, done and gotten out of the way, so they could concentrate on business matters. But to our mothers it was much more. My mother felt it was important to consult a reliable astrologer, to ensure the stars aligned and the match was a compatible one."

"Goodness! Just like mama!" Ava exclaimed.

"My parents, Shirinbai and Jalbhai were long-time friends of Homi's parents. My papa Jalbhai had made his fortune in South Africa, dealing in gold and diamonds. Homi's family in Bombay were of modest means. So, papa offered to undertake astrologer consultation."

"Oh!" Ava said, disappointed that history had repeated itself. Jer went on, "The appointment was made and mother followed papa to the astrologer's shabby office. As a very orthodox *Pundit*, he would not see mama's face so she was seated on the other side of the curtain that separated the astrologer and papa."

The astrologer examined Jer and Homi's horoscope charts.

Before he spoke, papa asked loudly, "It is a good match, right, right?"

Many years later, he told the story at a family dinner. He had silently nodded vigorously at the astrologer and pulled out a large roll of banknotes which he had handed over to the open-mouthed astrologer. Papa always laughed, saying the man had never seen that amount of money in years of reading horoscopes. Of course, the astrologer had heartily agreed with him and papa emerged from behind the curtain, looking pleased. He told my delighted mother to get whatever she needed for a lavish but quick wedding. He had to return to business in South Africa within a fortnight."

"Oh, Aunt Jer!" Ava exclaimed, trying to push away the thought that her dad might have the same idea as Jer's father.

No, she thought, he'd never do that to me.

But was she right? Was Dad getting rid of an obligation, or was he genuinely looking out for her happiness?

Perhaps he was eager that she should be well-settled, she decided, just not in the modern manner she would have preferred.

Punching and pummeling the dough helped vent her pent-up frustration. She rolled out the dough, sprinkling it generously with cinnamon, sugar mixed with a teaspoon of vanilla and a generous slathering of butter. Wiping her floured hands on her apron, she placed the buns, after they had risen, into the hot oven.

Baking usually quietened her mind, but not today. She had many unanswered questions and like a bee going from flower to flower collecting pollen, her mind needed to collect answers to the introductions she had taken part in and their results.

The fragrance of the baked cinnamon buns bursting with buttery goodness scented the air and tucking into them with a steaming cup of tea was just what she needed to dissipate the stress of the day and put a smile on their faces.

Chapter 10
The Party

At first glance Eruch's party looked tolerable, Ava thought. Eruch greeted them at the open door to his apartment, dressed in his usual white pants and shirt, unlike his colorfully attired guests.

"Welcome Homi and Ava," he said, ushering them in with a mock bow and a flourish of his left hand. They murmured their thanks.
"Ava, you look delicious," he whispered in her ear, while his right hand wandered down her back. She managed to stop his hand from going any further by firmly but politely grabbing his elbow and acting as if nothing untoward had happened.

She fixed a smile on her face and absentmindedly danced with a few eager young men, but since none caught her interest, they all melded into one boring lot. The living room was getting louder with jokes from inebriated men getting bolder as the evening wore on. Balloons were being bounced in the air and around the living room to much laughter. One of the balloons tapped Ava on the head and she playfully hit it back in the air towards eager hands waiting for it to come their way. Couples did their version of the rock and roll, while others gyrated to the twist and the ones disinclined to dance, clapped in rhythm to the loud music. An air of gay abandon was the mood of the party and Ava's initial reservations began to melt away as she found herself enjoying the lively mood and the dancers jiving the evening away.

Ava saw an obviously drunk woman slumped in the corner. Her tinted red hair kept falling onto her face. The green eyeshadow and bright red lipstick were smudged, giving her a sad clownish look. Ava felt a wave of pity for the woman who had obviously been beautiful at one time. A young man was tending to her, trying vainly to convince her not to have another drink. She abstractedly waved him aside, with her hand that held a cigarette, ash scattering around and on her red dress. The dress had a deep plunging neckline that showed off the jiggle of her bosom every time she moved. She seemed oblivious to her disheveled state as she downed another Scotch on the Rocks.

Nergish Lashkari, a neighbor and friend of Aunt Jer, spied Ava in the crowded room and made a beeline for her. Lowering herself heavily onto the sofa next to Ava, she whispered in the girl's ear as their gaze followed the titian-haired woman, "Do you know her?" she asked. Without waiting for an answer, she confided, "Her name is Ruby and she and Adil have a sad relationship."

"Who is Adil?" asked Ava perplexed.

"He is the gentleman tending to Ruby's whims!" Nergish replied, her eyes widening to emphasize her disapproval.

"How so?" asked Ava, trying to hide her disinterest.

"Well, ever since Ruby joined Air India she has morphed into a flashy, flibbertigibbet."

"What do you mean?" asked Ava, puzzled.

"Well, you know a flighty kind of person," said Nergish, slightly annoyed at being interrupted.

She paused to take a breath and then carried on, "their relationship ended a long time ago, but Adil seems to hang around her like a lost puppy." She sighed deeply, shaking her head while observing Ruby quickly down yet another drink.

Ava recognized him as the person Jer and Homi had spoken of with pitiful resignation about his dead-end relationship with Ruby. She remembered them saying that after Ruby had become a flight attendant, she had also become promiscuous, a smoker and wore excessive makeup. Basically, they had indicated that Ruby had had a 360-degree change in behavior.

Nergish, loving an audience for her gossip, carried on filling Ava in about Ruby and Adil.

"Adil has noticed everything about the way she has changed but hopes its a phase," she said rolling her eyes upwards and shaking her head. "This is no phase; she has undergone a total metamorphosis," she scoffed, as if this should be as plain as daylight to everybody.

Ava turned her gaze to the others in the room, hoping to either be rescued by a dancing partner or discreetly sending a message to Nergish that she was bored by this gossip. But Nergish was on a roll and putting her hand on Ava's arm, and looking sideways at the couple, she carried on in a low confiding tone, "Adil is patient to a fault and in this case, I think," she said after downing her snifter of brandy in one big gulp, "his patience with her really is his blind spot. This one-sided relationship has run out of love and been replaced by habit. I say it's time to cut the cord!" she said, her voice rising.

With a deep sigh and seemingly having off-loaded her stash of gossip, Nergish got up and went looking for another drink and the possibility of fresh gossip.

Ava let out a breath of relief at Nergish's exit, and went in search of Uncle Homi but got waylaid by Eruch, delighted at his opportunity to corral her.

What a figure! Eruch thought, wanting to be near her, to touch her. He found himself imagining her taut nipples under the chiffon of her dress. As she retreated, he admired her dainty feet in their gold, slinky, high-heeled sandals. But she was a frightened little thing, he thought as Ava stayed close to Homi, forcing Eruch to turn his attention to another guest.

Grudgingly Eruch let her go, his gaze following the sway of her hips and the long swanlike neck that he longed to ravish. He slowly undressed her in his thoughts and imagined her with her chiffon dress unzipped and slipping off her golden body.

Ava, the sickly child he'd seen on and off over the years had blossomed into a dazzling young woman. But she had that nonchalance that gave him a peculiar feeling. The little snob, what did she mean running off like that? He wanted her gazing up at him in admiration, no, in supplication! How could he make her subservient to him?

Stroking his thin moustache, he pondered how he could convince her that he was not a short, ugly, impotent, immigration officer, but rather someone of power. Someone she unquestionably needed. In his fantasy, she was wide-eyed, twisting her hands together, begging for his help.

"Oh Lord," thought Ava, "not this creep again." But it was his party Aunt Jer had asked her to attend, so when Eruch asked for a dance, she felt obligated to comply.

She could feel the perspiration coming through his shirt under her hand on his shoulder and his sweaty palm on her back. Feeling nauseous but remembering her manners she managed to grit her teeth into a smile and endured the spin around the dance floor. She saw Nergish from the corner of her eye and her chance to extricate herself from him.

"Eruch, please excuse me, I must speak with Nergish before she leaves the party."

Reluctantly, slowly, Eruch released her and watched as she went and sat next to a welcoming Nergish who had not found any salacious goings on and was happy to have Ava as her captive audience. Again, the older woman's gaze turned towards Adil.

"You know, Ava, Adil is the intelligent, strong, silent type. Self-sufficient and empathic, likely as a result of him being orphaned at an early age," she paused to take a sip of her drink.

Savoring her third glass, her tongue had loosened considerably. Nergish was bent on continuing to talk about Adil. Ava tried to escape by getting up and starting to walk away but felt Nergish's hand on her elbow, urging her to stay.

Ava looked around for Uncle Homi in the hope that they could exit the party, but he was nowhere to be seen.

Disinterested in Nergish's gossip but having Hobson's choice between a watchful Eruch on the prowl and a gossipy Nergish, she chose the latter and sat down, her hands restlessly smoothing over the silky fabric of the sofa.

Ava pressed the icy glass of Club Soda she was drinking to her warm cheek, to calm herself, watching the fizzy bubbles and the clink of the melting ice cubes as Nergish droned on about Adil.

"You know he has the street smarts needed to survive and flourish in this harsh Indian life. One would have expected him to be hardened by having seen the rough side of life but on the contrary he seems to have a big heart with empathy for those less fortunate than him."

Nergish was portraying a saint! thought Ava, itching to escape more of her droning on. But with a quick sip of her drink, the woman carried on talking.

"Ruby was the only girl he had been attracted to after they started dating, he seemed blind to all other women. Ruby's colleagues were very beautiful and tried again and again for Adil's attention but never succeeded."

Sighing heavily again and throwing up her hands, she grimaced and said, "Maybe he should have given them a chance!"

At this point Ava could not tolerate the gossip anymore.

She stood up and said with a finality, "Nergish, I am tired and famished!" and not waiting for a response, her chiffon dress floating like a cloud around her, quickly walked over to the next room where the food was laid out.

There were three tables. Two smaller ones at each end of the main long table. One end table held an assortment of appetizers. Mini samosas, delicate finger sandwiches and little skewers of chicken interspersed with squares of charred yellow bell peppers and tomatoes. The batik printed tablecloth covered the long table in the middle with brass dishes of various sizes and shapes glimmering with a sumptuous array of colorful kebabs, rich kormas, spicy curries and crisp cutlets. Complimenting this were platters of rice dishes, golden saffron, fluffy Basmati and Jasmine each steaming hot and fragrant.

The exotic dessert table stood separately at the other end of the large table, with heavy silver trays laden with *halva*[11], vermicelli garnished with slivered almonds, pistachios and raisins and assorted confectionaries flavored with rosewater.

The mingling of spicy and sweet aromas was intoxicating and delighted the senses. She could hear the hum of favorable comments about the delicious food from the guests around the table.

Adil was at the buffet table choosing delicacies Ruby had asked him to bring her. He had the resigned, defeated look of someone used to being ever obliging, without any reciprocation.

"If you really want her, why don't you stop chasing her?" Ava asked him. She was as stunned with her outburst as he was.

Horrified, she covered her mouth, wishing she could swallow her words. But like arrows escaping their quiver, there was no return.

They had seen each other in passing, at various functions but had never been introduced. She had not intended to say anything but seeing him behave in that subservient manner, with people whispering pitiful comments about his empty relationship with Ruby, had suddenly made her voice her outrage.

---

[11] sweetmeats

"Who are you?" asked Adil startled, with a look that seemed like he was seeing her through a fog, trying to figure out who she was... and then he looked at her again, noticing her for the very first time.

"What do you mean?" he asked.

"Well, if you stopped chasing her and bowing to her every command, she may show you some respect," Ava said, firmly, her chin held high.

She knew then that he understood what her comment meant. Ava blushed as his earnest brown eyes gazed at her for a few long minutes. Their surroundings and why they were even looking at each other seemed forgotten.

They avoided each other for the rest of the party. The last she saw of him that evening was the sight of him struggling to prop up a visibly drunk Ruby, in an effort to take her home.

Ava shrugged off the image, relieved to see Homi signaling her, that it was time to call it a night. Collecting her chiffon wrap and satin purse, she waved a goodbye to everyone, kissed Eruch on the cheek as briefly as she could and skipped into the elevator so fast that Homi had to catch up to her.

Just another party, she thought, yawning and looking forward to her large bed covered in soft linen. Later, as she drifted off to sleep, she remembered that lingering, haunted look in Adil's eyes.

Chapter 11
Nergish Lashkari

Nergish Lashkari, Jer's neighbor, lived in the flat directly below her, on the first floor of the building at Gowalia Tank. She had a roly-poly figure and wore her make up only on her face, not allowing it to go beyond her chin to her neck and décolleté. The result was that of a moon-like face on top of a fleshy neck.

She was spirited, upbeat and content with her lot in life, not allowing much to annoy her usually sunny disposition.

The one thing she was very possessive and sensitive about was the use of her phone. It was the only one in the entire building and she felt whomever she allowed to use it was obliged to divulge all details of the call. Inquisitive and eager for juicy gossip, the goings-on of others piqued her interest.

Nergish called out loudly, "Jer! Jer, phone!"

Jer's sandals quickly click-clacked over the marble-tiled floor to the back of the flat. There, an iron fence separated the two floors, through which Jer and Nergish exchanged word of phone calls.

Having a phone was a rare service in the 1960s in Bombay. Nergish's husband was a prominent lawyer in the metropolis and therefore able to get a precious landline telephone. Jer was one of the luckier neighbors whom Nergish allowed to use her phone.

Jer reached the back of the flat and replied, "Nergish dear, thank you, I will be right down."

"Jer dear, the phone call is for Ava."

"Oh gosh, Nergish, she has a bad case of laryngitis... but I will send her down right away," said Jer.

She flew into Ava's bedroom and said, "You have a call! Hurry downstairs to Nergish's flat. Wonder who it is?"

Ava rushed downstairs to the waiting Nergish, thanked her and picked up the phone.

"Hello," she said in a barely audible voice, expecting to hear her mother's instructions on where to meet for a visit to yet another matchmaker or hopefully to a new restaurant for dinner.

"Ava?"

"Yes, this is Ava, who am I speaking to?" she inquired in a hoarse whisper.

Even before she asked, she knew, but still would not allow herself to believe it could be him. It was Adil.

"Your voice sounds very different," he said hesitantly. "Sorry, I have laryngitis," said Ava.

"I love your voice... it sounds more wonderful with the huskiness of laryngitis... sorry, sorry, I did not mean to convey that I am glad your throat is sore," he said apologetically, then went on in a rush.

"Ava, I have been fighting within myself... I knew I had to speak with you... ask you if you would please consider meeting me. I really, really need to talk to you."

She could hear the urgent desperation in his voice. The battle within him must have been profound because at the party, he'd made a point of steadfastly avoiding her, choosing to tend to an intoxicated Ruby, oblivious to everyone present.

Ava did not know what to think, her thoughts were a whirlwind. She remained silent, hardly believing his words. Was this some sort of joke?

"Ava, are you still there?"

She finally found her voice, a raspy whisper, "I will think about it. I really don't know.

How did you get this phone number? Please do not call again, I must hang up now," she said as firmly as her voice would allow.

"Ava, please, please see me. I have been fighting the thought of calling you, since I first met you at Eruch's party a month ago. I desperately need to speak to you, please."

"I must get off the phone now. I just do not know and I am not well," Ava said, noticing Nergish giving her a quizzical look.

Goodness! What would she say to Nergish, who was expecting to hear all the details of her phone call? After all it was her phone line.

But Adil would not give up.

"I know it is difficult for you to receive phone calls at the Lashkaris, but may I please call you again in a few days? I am hoping you will be feeling better and agree to see me. Ava please," he pleaded.

"Goodbye, I must go now," she said and hung up.

Nergish, smiled expectantly as she led Ava down the long hallway.

"Well?" She prompted in anticipation.

"Thank you, Nergish," Ava replied, in a gravelly whisper. "What did they want?" Nergish demanded, raising her eyebrows.

The hallway had never seemed that long to Ava before.

She coughed delicately and pointed to her sore throat as she walked quickly to the door. Mouthing a silent thank you to Nergish, she went upstairs, hoping to tiptoe unnoticed to her bedroom. She wanted to be left alone with her thoughts after Adil's shocking phone call.

Her mind swirled with questions. How had Adil managed to get Nergish Lashkari's home phone number?

Why was he insistent on speaking to her?

She barely knew him and had not even been formally introduced. She flinched, remembering her startling comment to him at the party. Should she apologize?

Surely that did not require a meeting, she reasoned. It was just a phone call, but it left many puzzling questions.

Chapter 12
Adil

Adil Irani had grown up an orphan for most of his life. Both his parents had passed away when he was 10 years old. He took the place of his parents, as best he could, particularly with his younger brother, Freddy, who had been keenly affected by the loss of his parents, and had gone silent through the years. Adil had taken him under his wing.

With Adil's entrepreneurial skills, he had opened two juice shops which he ran, together with Freddy. Soon Adil was able to buy a car and a small but well-appointed flat, a rarity in the dearth of living-spaces in Bombay.

With his younger brother and himself on solid ground financially, Adil felt a huge weight come off his shoulders. A friend had introduced him to the world of body-building and he had immersed himself in it with enthusiasm and discipline. Soon he was at the top of the body-building scene, winning trophy after trophy, allowing his self-esteem to soar. His integrity remained intact and though he was lauded in the field and successful in the financial world, he remained grounded and humble.

Adil thought back to the conversation he had had with his older brother Rusi, a while ago...

Adil's car had been in the garage for repairs and Rusi, his elder brother had offered to pick him up from the juice shop and drop him off at his flat at Nariman Point. As Adil got into his car, Rusi had had the chance to have a one-on-one conversation with him.

"Adil with your university years fast approaching the end, do you think this is a good time to look around for a wife and settle down?" he asked with the hint of a smile.

"I love that you can really picture me with a family?" Adil had laughingly said, taken by surprise at his brother's suggestion.
"Well, why not, you have almost finished your degree in Biology and set yourself up in business?" his brother replied.
"Rusi, you know how often I have asked and been rebuffed in my marriage suggestions to Ruby?" replied Adil, morosely.

Rusi looked away, shaking his head and throwing up his hands in a despairing gesture. He had noticed the once promising but later dysfunctional relationship between Adil and Ruby over the years.
Gingerly broaching the subject, he asked quietly, "Where are you and Ruby at in your relationship?"
Even though he had known the answer to that question, he wondered if Adil had come to the realization that Ruby's intentions had become pretentious and self-serving.

Adil was grappling with finding the right words to convey the wretchedness of his relationship with Ruby.
Finally, he said bitterly, "Rusi, quite frankly, it's a train wreck. I am unsure of what to do!".

"Adil, you are strong and have overcome a mountain of adversities. I think you *know* what you need to do, just unwilling to take the necessary actions to get it done! "Rusi replied bluntly.

"Rusi, I have been courting Ruby since we were in university and had eyes for no other woman, you know that, right?" said Adil, hoping his brother would understand his attachment to Ruby.

"Adil, I can sugar coat the truth or I can tell you what I really feel are the facts, which do you prefer?" Rusi said in a direct, no-nonsense manner.

Rusi felt the responsibility of an older brother and father figure to Adil as well as their youngest brother. He was of the strong conviction that responsibility lay on his shoulders to steer both of his brothers in the right direction.

"Look, I know it's not an easy situation to be in and I am always here to help," he said gently, knowing he was in sensitive territory.

"I suggest you give your relationship with Ruby and your life in general, some serious introspection. Then, when you are ready, and you feel like talking about it, we can sit down and have a free and frank discussion about this." Rusi patted his brother on the shoulder, as he dropped him off at his flat.

"Sure, let's do that," Adil said, realizing that his brother had been more observant about his life, than he had thought.

Adil's youth had been a whirl off getting his body in shape for the next competition, getting together with his buddies at the gym, running his stores and cramming in his university studies. He was always eager to act on a wise business venture and pour his energy into it till it was profitable. Then he would share the daily running of it with his younger brother. There was no place or time for a woman in his life, let alone a wife and children, or so he had thought.

The day he set eyes on Ruby across the university courtyard, that thinking changed.

He had fallen head over heels for Ruby Shroff and his every waking thought was of her. Everything else in his life had taken a second place to her. Ruby was the most beautiful young woman he had ever seen. She had no shortage of suitors ready to please her every desire.

Adil as always, dedicated himself to being ahead of the pack. He wanted Ruby and pursued her with the same single-minded zeal that had brought him success in other pursuits in his life. Having Ruby exclusively to himself was his goal. Since she demanded virtually all his attention, the time-consuming daily discipline of body-building was dropped in favor of three rigorous weekly workouts at the gym. Soon, his friends hardly ever saw him without Ruby by his side.

He remembered pensively, the heady, romantic time of the university years with Ruby whose heart he had won. Then, they had eyes only for each other and life was a whirlwind of happy time spent together.

Thinking about when Ruby had switched from a sweet, intelligent, reserved girl to the woman she was today, he could not quite put his finger on the exact moment but felt it was around the time after university, when she was recruited by Air India as a flight attendant. That was when her keenness for marital bliss had turned instead, to the frequent comment of "What's the hurry!"

As the years after university progressed, Ruby would assure him with a kiss or a pat on the hand that, "Darling, of course we will marry!"

At the time he had gone along with her wishes, feeling certain that eventually she would be ready for marriage. The shift in their relationship had crept in so gradually that he had taken it as just a temporary phase of adjustment.

Chapter 13
Ruby

Riding in Adil's car with the window down and the breeze blowing her hair into a disheveled mess, Ruby threw her head back, eyes half closed and laughed with gay abandon. Since Adil admired her hair that way, she let it sway with the wind, while he smiled and tenderly held her hand.

Ruby was glad she would be moving out of her parents' humble flat. Remembering how despondent she had felt as she looked around the small room she shared with them, she had known she had to get out of there and find a way to live her dreams. After meeting Adil, she knew he was the ticket to her salvation and turning her dreams into a reality. She had imagined the luxury of living in Adil's fabulous flat overlooking the sea and she wanted it badly.

Though she would have gladly moved out of her parents' home and into Adil's flat in a flash, she knew biding her time for the right moment was the smarter way to go about it.

Ruby complimented herself on being shrewd, savvy and, though she loathed it… patient.

She had also known that marriage was part of the deal to achieve her goals. For the most part, she accepted it as the price one had to pay for an upscale lifestyle. Privately, she felt marriage was not all it was cracked up to be.

Well, comfort far outweighed reputation. Moving in before she eventually had to marry Adil would cause a huge scandal and disgrace her family, but... she did not care. After all she could see the type of marriage her parents had settled for. Examples of their sad mix of marriage, poor living standards and misery, were all around their home.

She had hoped her diligent attention to her studies and Adil's generosity would lift her out of her parents cramped flat and humble lifestyle.

Dressing to meet Adil, she put on a flowing white dress with tiny red polka-dots, clipped on large silver hoop earrings and slipped into strappy, silver high-heeled sandals. Twirling around and around in front of the mirror, admiring her reflection, she felt she had struck the note she wanted, a balance of conservatism with a touch of coy.

Adil was unlike anyone she had ever known. Tall, with a magnificent, muscular body, likely the result of his bodybuilding, he was also calm and dependable in demeanor. Ruby could hardly believe his unswerving loyalty to her. She knew how fortunate she was to have him in her life.

But she could not resist temptation. Even though she knew she was being fickle and reckless, she could not stop. She would flirt with the young men at the university campus, knowing she was upsetting Adil but she loved all the adulation that came her way and knew that Adil would calmly forgive her every time, professing his love for her.

She was aware Adil owned two shops and was planning to add more. He also owned his own flat and a fancy car. She had realized that for most people in this hard struggle of Bombay life, this counted as wealth.

In him, she had seen all her wildest dreams coming to fruition and it had made her dizzy with hope and happiness.

Chapter 14
Ruby Moves In

Adil stared at his cup of morning tea, remembering how it had all started so innocently.

He'd proposed to Ruby again, she had accepted his ring, so he was not surprised the next morning when the phone rang, that it was Ruby.

"Hello darling," Ruby said in her silky seductive voice, "I am still admiring the ring! I showed it to Mum and Dad and of course they were thrilled."

"Great, darling, so happy you liked it. I told the jeweler every gem had to be as flawlessly beautiful as you," Adil replied.

Ruby laughed.

"Darling, I am going to surprise you in a few minutes!"

Adil had felt pleased.

"Wonderful, can you give me a hint?"

"No, you will just have to be a little patient," she said evasively, a smile in her voice.

Adil did not have to wait long. Fifteen minutes later, Ruby came up the stairs to his flat followed by four sweaty men, each carrying loaded suitcases. A confounded Adil had opened the door as Ruby swept past him instructing the men on where to place the bags in his flat.

After she had paid and dismissed the men, she went over to Adil, sat him down and jumped onto his lap, wrapping herself around him in a long hug and kiss.

"Hope you like your surprise!" she said pointing at the suitcases.
"I am moving in with you."

Adil felt stunned. He had assumed that she would move in after they were married.

"Ruby darling, when did you decide all this?

Should we not wait until we get married or at the very least discuss it?" he asked.

Ruby seemed nonchalant about what the neighbors or her parents would think of her living with a man before marriage.

"I know it will be quite the scandal, but really Adil, I don't care! I'm fed up staying in my parents' tight quarters!

"Adil sweetie, you did say you would do anything to please me, right?" she said with a pout.

Adil felt disturbed at the order in which things had suddenly progressed, but he had in fact said that he would do anything to please her.

So, he asked, "Ruby darling, have you really thought this through? Let us get married as soon as possible and then you move in. This is going to upset your parents. You don't want everyone gossiping, do you?"

"Well, Adil, I really don't care about all the tongue wagging and as far as mum and dad are concerned, they will get over it," Ruby said in a dismissive way.

"Anyway, I cannot marry you soon," she announced, in a matter-of-fact manner.

Adil felt bewildered. "Why ever not?"

She grinned as she traced her finger down his arm.

"I've decided to become a flight attendant with Air India and they have promised me international routes. Married women can't be stewardesses, did you know?

"Anyway, what is the hurry to marry, darling, let me see the world for a while and then we can settle down. Meanwhile whenever

I am in town, I will stay right here with you. Isn't that fantastic?" she cooed.

"No, I do not think it's fantastic, Ruby," he said, confused.

"After all these years of waiting to settle down you are now saying you have decided to become a flight attendant?

Why did we just get engaged if not to marry?"

"Oh relax, honey, of course we will eventually get married, you know we will, right?" she had said blowing him air kisses.

Chapter 15
Ruby the Flight Attendant

The conversation had never really happened, Adil realized as he drove to work. The years had swiftly gone by, and Ruby slipped away from his suggestions to 'have an honest talk' with a sassy smile, or an excuse that she was tired.

Adil turned thirty-two years old and yearned to settle down and have a family life. But Ruby who was the same age showed no sign of tiring of her high-flying job as an international flight attendant. Ruby seemed intoxicated with the international flights, new sights and cuisines, meeting new people and the mile-high club lifestyle. Life was fast paced and exciting and Ruby took to it like a duck to water. This was a semblance of life she pictured having for herself and she was determined to juice it for all it was worth.

Adil disliked her long absences away from home but Ruby was elated at travelling the globe, with an enhanced and bolder sense of confidence.

"Ruby darling, does the thought of endless travelling; the different hotels and time differences tire you?"

"Wishful thinking sweetheart, I could go on travelling forever and love every minute of it. It feels less like work and more like endless adventures."

Ruby had gradually become more independent of Adil and their relationship was changing slowly but surely, with the shifting sands of time.

Lighting a new cigarette from the previous butt, she inhaled deeply and picked a piece of tobacco from her mouth as she leisurely blew rings of smoke into the air. Checking her make-up in the mirror... green eyeshadow, rouged cheeks, scarlet red lipstick, darkly lined eyes with false eyelashes... she was pleased with the result.

This was the new Ruby, the flight attendant. The old Ruby with her glowing natural beauty and sweet radiant smile had been replaced by heavy makeup, the lingering stench of cigarettes and a worldly knowing look.

The phone rang, shrill in the relative quiet of 2 am. Adil sleepily groped for the phone but Ruby jumped up like a cat and grabbed the phone before he could. From the conversation he overheard and her strange behavior he suspected it was a new admirer.

Lately, there had been many of these calls that Ruby had refused to allow him to answer and was elusive about who they were from. "Just friends..." she would say evasively but her smug smile indicated the person was much more than a friend.

He realized that he and Ruby had fallen into a dull routine. He would pick her up at the airport when she arrived, drive her to her parents where she would unload their gifts, and then on to his flat where she would pour herself a glass of Scotch whisky and kick off her high heeled pumps. After a few glasses of Scotch, she would fall asleep on the sofa where she was sitting. Adil would carry her to bed or cover her with a soft blanket on the couch and go to bed. He felt protective and loved watching her sleep. She looked like the girl he fell in love with, sweet innocence in repose.

In fact, he was grudgingly coming to the realization that love was a thing of the past as there was no reciprocity and he had become a caregiver rather than her fiancé. The change in her had come about very gradually, but she had changed for sure. Ruby did as she wished, certain that Adil would pick up the pieces. Later that day, he acknowledged with a wry smile that he was a fool. She could do the most unforgivable things to him and then seduce him into forgiving her.

Adil shook his head in frustration. Each time he broached the subject of marriage, she would convince him that it would happen soon. Just a few more exotic destinations to see "Hawaii, darling! I just have to see Hawaii!" and then she would settle down with him. She seemed to have no intention of keeping her word or moving out of his flat.

Adil realized, with a weary sigh, that he'd been placated many times and allowed her to carry on living as she wished. She liked having a spacious beautifully decorated flat to come home to. Adil was always there to pick her up from the airport and take her wherever she wished. Though he did not smoke and drank lightly at social functions only, Adil had even come around to accepting her penchant for whisky and cigarettes. Ruby was content with the status quo.

Adil was deeply unhappy. He thought he'd all but forgotten how to feel happy. He had invested over a decade in his love for Ruby and thought giving in to her wishes would eventually grow into a settled family life.

He looked at the piles of paperwork on his desk that needed his attention but felt too unhappy to tackle any work. Emptiness gnawed at his gut with the knowledge that the present Ruby was not the person he had fallen in love with. Adil was keenly aware that their relationship had been on the rocks for several years. He despaired that there had been a startling change in Ruby's behavior, but did not know how to get out of this unhappy situation. The fact that she had moved into his flat and had nowhere else to go except moving back in with her parents, made any change even more fraught with problems.

With a heavy heart, Adil drove to meet his brother Rusi for a heart-to-heart chat. Parking the car in the driveway of Rusi's office, he lifted the heavy knocker on the door. Rusi opened the door with a broad smile and a warm hug.

"Hi Rusi, how are you?"

"I am well but you do not look so hot!"

"I know, I know, to be honest I feel like hell!"

"What is the problem, brother? You know between us we can find a solution to the most difficult of problems, right?" he said patting Adil reassuringly on the back.

"Rusi, I hate to admit it but Ruby and I seem to be on separate paths," he said sitting down with his head in his hands.

"That may be a surprise to you Adil, but others have noticed that for a very long time..."

"What do you mean by "a long time?"

"Well, quite frankly it's been years. You just seem to have turned a blind eye to the changes in Ruby, but everyone else seems to have taken note."

"And what is the consensus, since "everyone seems to have taken note?"

"Well, brother, we all feel sorry for you."

"I do not want to be pitied for God's sake; I am a man not an invalid!" Adil exclaimed with indignation.

"Then behave like one! Stop being her fetch and carry boy! Can't you see she is using you like a public convenience?"

"Enough Rusi, this is too large a dose of reality," he gulped and put his hand up to stop his brother from speaking.

"Adil, you are being used as a lackey by Ruby, stop being walked all over and man up to this messy situation."

"What does my wise brother Rusi suggest?" asked a humbled Adil.

"You won't like my suggestion, but I will give it to you with great love. Make a clean break with Ruby, move her out of your flat and then with a clean slate and peace of mind you can hopefully find yourself a decent young lady to settle down with. That, my brother, is my strong suggestion to you."

"You offer sage advice brother, I will give you that, but.... difficult to put into action. Ruby took it upon herself to move in and will behave like a bobcat if I try to move her out."

"I do not doubt it, but it has to be done. This situation is depriving you of well-deserved happiness... Look, when you first met Ruby, you could not know it would turn out the way it has. Its best for both of you to go your separate ways. Yes, she will kick and scream, but find a way to move her out of your home and life."

"Rusi, I agree with your insight and suggestion," Adil said feeling nervously optimistic.

Rusi looked at his brother for a long time and squeezed Adil's shoulder.

"Remember I am always here for you," he said with a reassuring smile.

Adil hesitated and then said, "Rusi, there is one other matter."
"What is that?"

"I met a young lady at Eruch's party and cannot get her out of my mind."

"That is the most unusual remark I have ever heard from you..."

"Rusi, her name is Ava and she is here from South Africa."

"I have heard of her through my wife, said Rusi. I am told she is a beautiful person. Very classy and ready to settle down... this is good news... you finally, finally, have someone other than Ruby on your mind."

"Rusi, I hate to say this but after Ruby, I have found it difficult to trust my judgement. However, I have never felt surer of anyone other than yourself, as I feel about her. It does not make logical sense because I have not had the opportunity to get to really know her."

"So, why Ava? What is so special about her that you have not seen in a zillion other woman?"

"It's a gut feeling... that is all I have to go on at this time Rusi, but it is a very strong feeling. There is undoubtedly something genuine and earthy that draws me to her. I have tried to resist and failed."

"There is no need to resist, Adil. I suggest you go forward with this gut feeling and see where it leads you... Have courage brother... happiness will find you!" said Rusi encouragingly.

Chapter 16
Adil's Phone Calls

Ava frowned. After several phone calls in quick succession from Adil, her aunt's neighbor Nergish, had become increasingly agitated. Even Aunt Jer agreed that Nergish was becoming impatient with the repeated phone calls.

"Ava! Nergish is obliging us with one phone call a month or two at the most. These daily phone calls week after week is just too much!"
"I'm sorry, Aunt Jer, I can't help it. He just keeps calling!" said a frustrated Ava.

Jer's lips tightened. "Nergish told me very firmly that this is causing her migraines to flare up and she will not allow this to go on. I apologized profusely and assured her it would not continue."

Ava sighed; she did not have a clue on how to stop Adil from calling. She suspected that Nergish was miffed because she had not offered any information on who the calls were from or why they were so frequent. Daily phone calls and not a smidgen of gossip shared! Nergish rolled her eyes to the heavens.

Ava knew from the disapproval stamped on Aunt Jer's face that the phone calls could not continue. She also guessed that Adil would not stop phoning until she agreed to meet him.

She made a decision—she would agree to meet Adil once and hear him out.

It would be matter of fact, unemotional and to the point, she decided. Mama and Papa need not know. But how could she explain her decision to Aunt Jer?

It would likely be met with annoyance. Her guess was right.

Going downstairs to speak to Nergish, she practiced what she was going to say to placate her. She rang the bell and Nergish opened the door with a forced smile.

Ava said, sincerely, "Nergish I hope you will accept my apologies for the phone calls, I am really sorry, even though I have discouraged them."

Pausing for a moment and taking a deep breath, she continued, "Nergish I am going to ask you for a favor in order to stop this going on... I am asking that you allow me to receive one more call, which I guess will be tomorrow. I promise I will not ask for any favors after that."

Nergish frowned, looking down and away, a vein in her forehead pulsated, while Ava waited frozen into silence. After reflection, Nergish lifted her gaze and seeing the apologetic look on Ava's face, nodded. "One call and then peace? That seems all right." Her frown disappeared and was replaced by her moon face beaming a huge smile as she pressed Ava's hands in affirmation.

"Thank you, dear Nergish, thank you for your understanding," Ava said relieved.

Nergish continued smiling as she escorted her to the entrance. Ava took the stairs two at a time with an overwhelming sense of relief.

As expected, Adil called the next day, politely asking to speak to Ava.

"Ava!" Nergish called. "Phone!"

Ava was waiting for this call and fueled by anticipation and morning energy, she bounced down the stairs.

"Thank you, thank you Nergish, I will be right down," Ava called out.

Nergish ushered her down the long hallway, smiling.

"It sounds like the person on the phone is rather smitten with you, Ava. He's very persevering, isn't he!" she said suggestively.

Predictably, the call was from Adil, begging her to meet him 'to talk' as he put it.

"Adil, I will agree to meet you, once and once only, is that clear?"

"Yes, yes!" agreed Adil, elated.

"Adil, you know I am here with my parents who intend to introduce me to suitable marriage partners. I will not do anything to cause them concern. Do you understand?"

"Yes, yes, I understand."

"Choose a discreet place to meet and talk and remember its once only," she said firmly.

Adil agreed to everything she suggested, confirming a day, time and place for their rendezvous. She also informed him about her agreement with Nergish regarding any future phone calls.

Adil was silent.

Chapter 17
First Meeting with Adil

Ava dressed simply in a navy voile shirt and navy cotton pants. As she looped a thin silver belt into her pant waistline, she checked her reflection in the mirror. Satisfied with the no- nonsense, practical outfit she had chosen, she slipped on a pair of flat suede leather sandals and picked up her purse. Kissing Aunt Jer on the cheek, she promised to be home soon.

The moment her delicate sandals hit the pavement, the heavens opened up and the long-dreaded monsoon rains, came pouring down. She jumped into the taxi as sheets of rain soaked the hot, parched earth. She had dreaded the arrival of the monsoons and had hoped to be gone from Bombay before they arrived. Large pools of water bordered each road, making streets narrower, so that each car threw up a slush of muck on to pedestrians and there were traffic gridlocks at every intersection.

In the minutes it took to switch from the taxi to Adil's waiting car, her carefully put together outfit was soaking wet. Her hair which she had up in an elegant French twist, had come undone, drooping with frizzy tendrils. She wore no make-up and her golden skin glittered with lingering raindrops.

In his car, Adil and Ava sat looking at each other silently for what seemed like an eternity. They both realized they were totally alone for the very first time. They had never been alone before and now neither seemed to know what to say. He was shy and seemed lost for words. Finally, he broke into a grin.

"What is so funny?" Ava asked, knowing she looked disheveled.

"You look so cute with raindrops on your nose and hair," he said smiling.

"Cute, my foot. I look a mess. The monsoons had to begin today!" Ava said, annoyed that she was caught looking anything but perfect.

"Ava, you look beautiful, and I think the glistening raindrops enhance your natural beauty."

Ava shifted uncomfortably in her seat and said nothing.

"What would you like for dinner?" he asked.

"I am not hungry, so perhaps pick up some take-out food that you would like," Ava replied.

Adil disappeared into a restaurant bringing back with him two large brown paper bags. He drove in silence, parked the car and opened her door, inviting her upstairs to his flat.

She stepped into his flat and forgot all about her wet clothes and her fast-frizzing hair. The apartment was like a little hidden gem, a sanctuary from the hot, dirty, dusty and now rainy streets. Quiet and airy, with an exquisite view of the sea, it took her breath away. She felt a deep sense of peace and belonging.

She was startled by Adil's voice.

"Would you like me to lend you a clean shirt, while your blouse dries out?"

"No, no, I am fine, thank you," Ava replied, wrapping her arms tighter around herself. Without a word, Adil brought a large fluffy, sweet-smelling towel and silently draped it around her shoulders. He laid the dining table with two sets of plates, forks, knives, crisp napkins and moist towelettes from the neat kitchen. Then seating her and carefully pushing her chair in place, sat down across from her, and opened the packages, bringing forth tandoori chicken, salad and bottles of sparkling water and mango juice.

Adil and Ava sat silently for a while. Then she looked up at him, hoping he was not looking at her. He was looking at her, intently. Neither had touched their food. A strong current of emotion flooded through her. Ava tried to look away... but found herself gazing into his soulful brown eyes. What she saw was heart wrenching honesty, mixed with surprise at his feelings.

Faced with being alone with Adil, without another person to divert his attention, she expected to feel uncomfortable. Much to her surprise, she felt none. Instead, a feeling of total peace came over her, as if she had been on a long journey and had finally come home.

"Ava, I hardly know what to say," Adil said.

"I have never asked to date anyone in my whole life, other than Ruby."

He continued, "She knows there is nothing left between us, except habit. I should have broken it off with her several years ago... she was almost always away... and when she was here, I just did not want to quarrel."

"Quarrel about what?" Ava asked.

"Asking her to move out of this flat, finally breaking up with her, recognizing the end of the relationship..."

He shifted uncomfortably in his chair, looking around uneasily.

"Ava as I am speaking to you, I realize this sounds unacceptable and I admit I have been avoiding a confrontation with Ruby. I will be speaking with her as soon as she arrives back from New York."

He had not touched his food but had taken gulps of the sparkling water at various intervals, as if it would help him convey his thoughts.

Ava nodded thinking if she'd moved in with a man, her father would have disowned her publicly!

Adil said, "Ava, I do not know why... I was extremely, attracted to you. Please, don't misunderstand me, you are undoubtedly beautiful. The surprising thing that I cannot explain, even to myself, is that I have come across many alluring women, in fact some of Ruby's colleagues have openly flirted with me. I have never found myself even remotely interested."

As he spoke, she saw no signs of guile, just simple honesty.

"With you, the moment you spoke to me, it was like I had finally come out of a long coma. I was astonished that I could want to get to know you so keenly. This was a strange feeling for me. I met you a few times afterwards at parties and deliberately avoided you. I was hoping the strong attraction to you would go away."

Ava felt bewildered at his candor. He gave a nervous laugh.

"I really tried to deny my feelings, but they were so intense, that I surprised myself by going to great lengths to find a phone number where I could reach you." He looked earnest, "I could not think of another way of reaching you. Please accept my apologies for the inconvenience. I did offer my apologies to Nergish but she still sounded very bothered."

Ava had planned to hear out Adil and tell him that there was no chance of meeting again. Instead, she found herself enjoying his company, and finding credibility in what Adil said. Being with him, felt like the most natural thing in the world. This was not supposed to happen! She reminded herself to be sensible. However, it seemed her sensible self... had deserted her.

She cautiously looked up at him, while sipping her mango juice. Their gaze floating to one another, met and locked, neither could look away. His eyes were full of a shy, surprised love. Finally, she looked away, wanting to hide her feelings which were undoing all her saner intentions.

"I think it's time to go home," she suggested while averting his gaze.

He pulled the curtains aside and looked out onto the deserted street.

"The rain is still coming down heavily, I think it's prudent to wait until it has subsided," he replied.

She silently nodded, knowing what he said made sense. She acknowledged to herself, that she was glad she had a perfectly logical reason to delay her departure.

"Would you like to listen to some music? I don't know what your tastes are but do have a look at what I have here. There may be something you like," Adil suggested.

Almost immediately she spotted a song she loved and asked him to play it for her. Soon Diana Ross's sultry voice sounded through the flat, "Touch me in the morning." Ava softly hummed along with it, "Touch me in the morning... then just walk away... leave me as you found me... empty as before."

Adil looked mesmerized, admiring her, while she enjoyed the music and lyrics. She asked him to play it over and over again and he happily obliged. She felt the words of that song would stay in her memory forever.

When the rain finally abated to a gentle shower, they both knew it was time to go home.

Adil gently held her hand and asked, "Ava, please say you will see me again. Please Ava, this evening has been the happiest I have ever been in decades."

"Adil, you should not have to beg anyone to be with you," Ava said. "I came here tonight expecting to see you *once*, so that you would not upset Nergish and Aunt Jer by your phone calls."

"I know you only agreed to see me this one time and it's selfish of me to ask for more... I hope you understand, I need you, Ava," he said, his face flushed.

Ava wrung her hands, feeling absurdly nervous about seeing him again. Her mind raced with unanswered questions. Being accustomed to the discipline of hiding her feelings, she straightened her back and composed herself. Lightly placing one hand upon the other and removing the worried look from her face, she steeled herself to be calm.

She continued in a soft voice, "I would like to think about it, and discuss this with my parents and Aunt Jer... I do not want to give you false hope." His anxiety changed to a look of relief.

Picking her up in his arms, he whirled her around with joy. Finally, he gently put her down, took her face in his hands and looking into her eyes, said "Thank you, take all the counsel you need, but please remember... I need you in my life."

She thought she saw a tear in his eye, but did not comment because she felt close to tears herself.

He held her hand as they went down the stairs. There, Ava saw that water had filled the street, and crept up over the bottom two stairs.

"Please permit me," Adil said, as he carried her from the stairs to the car, avoiding her having to slosh through knee high rainwater that had pooled at the foot of the stairs.

They drove home in silence, with a realization something wondrous had happened that evening that could very possibly change the path of their lives, forever. It was a daunting but amazing feeling, like walking on a fluffy pink cloud, with angels smiling at you.

Chapter 18
Happy Time

They had agreed to meet two days later, on a Thursday, at 7pm. Ava wanted to try and think things through and clear her head. A sixth sense seemed to insist that this man was her soulmate.

How could it be? She barely knew him!

Adil was not the type of man she would likely be attracted to, let alone want to share her life with.

Her parents expected her to marry a doctor with a good income and high social status, of a well-known lineage, conforming to their social standing. She too admired people who were well read, highly educated, and easy to converse with. After all, her siblings had managed to marry into a family her parents approved of. What would she say to them?

If she said she was very much in love with him, there would be a hundred questions, she thought.

How do you know him? What's his education, financial standing and on and on?

Trying to find some fault with him, she talked to Aunt Jer about Adil.

"Well, dear one," Jer said, "In all the years Homi (Jers husband) and I have known him, there is absolutely nothing negative we could say about him," she paused, and then added "except..."

Ava felt her heart jerk in her chest. "Except what? Aunt Jer, please tell me, do not hide anything from me, be brutally honest."

"The only negative thing I can think of is his association with Ruby," Jer said, raised eyebrows underlining her disapproval.

"Ava, Ruby will likely go crazy when she hears about you meeting Adil."

The next day Ava prepared for her evening with Adil with excitement and a little trepidation. She decided on a blush pink silk blouse and skirt to match. The only jewelry she wore were pearl earrings and a watch. Her hair was pinned back and fell in soft waves around her face. As she stopped for a second to inspect her reflection in the hallway mirror, she saw a lovely young lady, nervously happy.

Hearing a distinctive beep, beep, of a car's horn, she looked out of the window to the street. Adil's smiling face appeared at his car window, looking up at her. She waved, and saying her goodbyes to Aunt Jer and Uncle Homi, ran downstairs.

Adil stood holding the car door open for her. They exchanged a smile, and he looked at her admiringly and with such love that it made her feel that her sixth sense was right.

He gently held her hand as he drove in silence, frequently turning to look at her with that same look of love and happiness.

At Juhu Beach, they got out of the car.

Together, they strolled along the beach, saying nothing, deeply content to be holding hands and being together. The early moon was full and golden, playing hide and seek among the clouds. It cast its glorious magic on the water, and the two happy lovers, deeply engrossed in their first kiss.

The world, time and place were forgotten. Ava felt she was floating on a cloud of joy. She was really surprised by how she felt about Adil. Everything was happening so fast; she could hardly believe it was real. She had never felt this sort of happiness before. Some presentiment warned her that she never would, with anyone else. Palms trees waved in the soft breeze and Ava savored each moment, blissfully happy.

"Ava," Adil sighed, looking at his watch. "It's time I took you home."

He opened the car door for her, thoughtfully tucked her skirt in and shut the door. As he started the car and put the gear into drive, he made a brief sound of exclamation.

"I almost forgot! That intoxicating fragrance reminded me." He looked at Ava apologetically.

"Is something the matter?" Ava asked feeling uneasy.

Leaning over, he pulled out a small box, opened it and gave it to Ava. Right away the hypnotically beautiful fragrance of gardenias flooded the car.

He said, "I brought these for you. Sorry, I forgot to give it to you at the beginning of the evening, will you accept it now?"

"Adil," Ava put her finger on his lips to stop his apologies, "They are exquisite, thank you."

She pinned the velvety white fragrant flowers in her hair and he sat looking at her loveliness, wishing he could rewind the whole evening. Gazing at her he knew with a certainty that came from somewhere deep in him, that this was the girl for him. It had come upon him so quickly, but this was real. He loved Ava and wanted her to be his life partner. How he could be so profoundly sure he did not know. The fragrant flowers in her hair, the luster of the pearls in her delicate ear lobes, the soft silk clothes that seemed to suit her soft, sweet demeanor... God, he adored her beyond words.

Time was slipping away and not wanting to earn Aunt Jer's wrath, keeping her out late, he tore his eyes away from her and put the car into drive, enjoying the feel of her hand in his, so dainty, soft, warm and loving.

"When will I see you again, Ava?"

"When do you want to see me again?" she asked with a smile.

Adil could not hold back. With Ava, he felt no hesitation. Feeling safe, assured in her affection that shone from her shy smile, he said,

"I want to see you the first thing in the morning when I awake and the last thing I see before I fall asleep. Ava, you have come into my life and made me know love, like I have never known it existed before. I'll want you with me, forever."

"Are you sure Adil? You hardly know me."

"I am profoundly certain, Ava. I would be honored if you would be my wife. I know I am not on my knees and do not have a ring for your finger, but I love you."

Ava felt like she wanted to jump up and down and say "Yes, yes, I will marry you." She did not know where this profound love came from. All she knew is it was there, with unshakeable certainty. No doubts at all. But she hardly knew him!

Her sensible side won out and she said after a long silence, and caution in her voice.

"You have not forgotten about Ruby, have you?"

She felt the rise of tension in him, and the tired, beaten down look return at the mention of Ruby.

He only said, "Ava, darling, I am sure. I realize you must need some time to think things through. I also must ask your dad for your hand in marriage. And of course, I must speak to Ruby when she arrives." he continued, the tired look replaced with one of optimism.

Ava smiled, "Shall we take it one step at a time, Adil?"

"I do not want to lose you Ava; I do not want to lose you."

They had long reached Jer's building but lingered, neither wanting the evening to end.

Ava took his face in her hands, looked him in the eyes and said, "You will not lose me," paused and then continued, teasing "unless you want to lose me!"

Finally, she broke away gently, waved, blew him a kiss and ran up the stairs. Aunt Jer awakened from dozing on the sofa, saw the look on Ava's face, and rolled her eyes upwards to the heavens. She had recognized the walking-on-air look of a woman in love, and Ava had all the unmistakable signs. Lord! Jer thought, alarmed, of all the young men in Bombay did Ava have to fall for Adil?

She wordlessly kissed Ava goodnight and headed to bed, waves of unease rippling through her.

Ava found it difficult to sleep, too excited with the whirl of events that had taken place that night. Hugging her pillow, she smiled at the moonbeams slanting across her bed, eventually falling into a deeply contented sleep, dreaming of being wrapped in the magic of Adil.

Ava was uncomfortable with Ruby being away and not being able to clear things with her right away. However, Adil had assured her that as soon as Ruby arrived and had rested, he would sit down and talk to her. He felt sure that she would initially make a fuss but eventually admit that there was nothing left in their relationship. They both knew they had long grown out of it.

If she was adamant about not leaving the flat, then he would gift it to her, instead of having a long-drawn-out battle over it. On some level he knew that Ruby valued ownership of the flat far more than she valued him. He was aware of how expensive the flat was and the years of hard saving he had to endure to afford it but... if that is what it took to cut ties with Ruby, he was now ready to get it done. He thought of the years of happiness lost because he had refused to believe Ruby did not love him enough to make a long-term commitment.

He would make it right, he thought, which was to give Ruby what she wanted... the beautifully appointed flat. He in turn hoped it would give him a chance at happiness with Ava.

Would this satisfy Ruby?

He felt restless and impatient awaiting Ruby's return from New York.

With even the faintest of hope of a future with Ava on the horizon, he suddenly felt he just could not wait any longer to uncouple himself from Ruby. He remembered his brother Rusi's advice on ending his relationship with Ruby. He wished he had acted much sooner, but he had not been ready. Now he was sure, and without doubt or uncertainty shadowing him.

Ava having spoken to Aunt Jer and Uncle Homi about her unexpected reaction to Adil's proposition that they meet again, felt it time to consult her mum.

Her usual confidence in her convictions had frayed and was teetering on indecision.

She went downstairs to reluctantly use Nergish's phone, taking with her a peace offering of apricot jam tarts she had baked. She had made them from her precious stash of All Gold brand South African jam. They looked like jewels on the ice clear glass plate.

"Ava these tarts look yummy. I will enjoy them later at tea time... on second thoughts that is too long to wait, I am going to have one right now!"

There was a momentary silence, "Mumm! absolutely delicious," Nergish said through her tart-stuffed mouth.

She finally left her alone with the tacit understanding that Ava needed privacy, disappearing down the long hallway into one of the many rooms, straining her ears to eavesdrop. She had overheard enough of Ava's conversations to be intrigued. To Nergish it was like the scent of blood to a hound. Ava sighed suspecting she was being listened to and dialed her mother's phone number.

"Ava!" answered her mother, first with delight and then trepidation.

"Is something wrong?"

"No, Ma, all is well but I was wondering if we could meet and have a chat?"

"Sure, sure darling, when shall we meet?"

"How about tomorrow, the Sea Lounge at the Taj?"

"That sounds fine Ava, around one o'clock for lunch?"

"Don't bring Dad please, let it be just us, okay?"

"Okay Ava darling, see you then," Dina said lightly, trying to hide her apprehension.

"Bye Ma," Ava said and hung up, guessing that Nergish would almost immediately appear and wondered how much she had heard.

Nergish came into the hallway right on cue, lifting her head with a smile encouraging conversation, but Ava was in no mood for chit chat.

Escaping Nergish and slowly climbing the stairs, she was deep in thought about meeting her mother and her response to the expected rat-a-tat-tat of a thousand questions.

Ava had a restless night, finally giving up the fight with her by now rumpled sheets. Slipping on a silk wrap against the night chill, she went to the one place that always managed to calm her, the bay windows fringing the hallway. The pre-dawn air refreshed her, easing her restlessness.

Returning to bed, she slept till the sun was high in the sky.

Chapter 19
Ava's Meeting with her mother

The next morning, she was awoken by Aunt Jer gently patting her shoulder with a reminder of the meeting with Dina. The sleep had restored her and she sprang into action hurriedly showering and dressing in cool white linen pants and a navy striped cap-sleeved blouse. She added a wide white straw hat and sunglasses to complete the look she sought.

Politely waving aside Aunt Jer's offer of a late breakfast, she raced down the stairs into the blinding sunshine.

Gowalia Tank was crawling with a mass of activity. Beggars calling to every passerby, cars honking ceaselessly in the impossible traffic jams, all manner of human forms pushing determinedly forward on the way to their destinations. Wandering idly in the midst of all this frenetic movement were the sacred garlanded cows.

She jumped into one of the many taxis circled around Gowalia Tank and instructed the Sikh driver to take her to the Taj Hotel. Throwing up her hands in despair as he proceeded to join the hooting cars and zig zag his way through the traffic, she sank into her seat turning her thoughts to her mother.

The taxi cruised to a smooth stop outside the Taj as Ava paid the driver and stepped onto the plush red carpet. The Taj hotel was her secret oasis in Bombay. When the chaos of life in Bombay overwhelmed her, she sought respite in its stately, well- ordered, classy lounges. Here she felt wrapped in its care to detail and pampered with invisible waiters providing brisk and efficient service. Ava feeling enveloped in luxury and a calm sense of order, breathed a satisfied sigh as the elevator lifted her up to the serenity of the Sea Lounge.

She spotted her mother waiting for her at a table next to the window overlooking the Arabian Sea. For a moment she was transported to the view from her home on the hill of Clarence Road. The sea changing daily from choppy little white-capped waves to smooth turquoise tranquility.

Ava removed her sunglasses and hat and hugged her mother. She seated herself, surveying the room with silent approval and delight.

"Ma, shall we order first and then chat?" Ava both questioned and suggested.

Dina keen to know what was on Ava's mind, nodded in agreement, looking forward to getting the ordering out of the way. A waiter appeared seemingly out of nowhere and they both ordered the shrimp salad and a large bottle of Perrier.

"So, Ava," said her mother leaning forward. "What is on your mind, dear one?"

"Mum, please promise me you will not freak out or make a scene?"

"Oh! My, is it that bad?"

"Nothing is bad, mum. In fact, it's good..."

"So, don't keep me in suspense... what is this good news, tell me, tell me?"

"I met someone; I really like him," she paused trying to choose her words carefully.

"He seems very different from most of the young men you have introduced me to."

"Oh, I knew it, I knew it. I even told your dad I had a feeling you clicked with one the twins you met last week!" Dina clapped her hands with glee and pinched Ava's cheek affectionately.

"Ma, now please don't get carried away, I did not like either of the twins. They were milksops just like all the others!"

Her mother frowned. "What are you talking about, Ava? I saw the two of you sharing a laugh in the corner of the living room... more importantly, remember they come from a prestigious family," she said punching the air with her fork and looking intently at Ava to see if her words had affected her daughter.

Ava bit her lip, then forged ahead.

"Ma, this person is someone I met at Eruch's party and he is the only young man that has sparked my interest since we came to Bombay an eternity ago!"

She very much wanted to share the latest happening in her life with her dear mother, and get her opinion on how to navigate these unknown waters, but trying to communicate on this subject was like picking your way between landmines, she thought wearily.

She'd begun to regret the idea of having a heart to heart with her mother. They seemed to be on two different planets!

"Ma, I wanted to share and get your advice on how to proceed next," she hesitated on whether to continue, but decided she did want her mother on board especially because of the Ruby conundrum.

"Mum, look I am going to be frank with you and I would like your opinion, I really value it, Ma..."

Furrowed brows and a look of serious concern came over Dina's face. Sensing that Ava was troubled, she gave her full attention to her.

"Mum, the young man is not from a prestigious lineage, but like dad a self-made man, comfortably wealthy, educated and very decent," Ava ventured.

"Hmmm, and how do you know the background of this person?" questioned her mother, eyebrows raised with concern.

"Well, Aunt Jer and Uncle Homi have known about him for some years and they agree that he is wonderful man."

"I see... so, why has Jer and Homi not introduced him earlier?"

"Uh... he has been kind of involved with a lady named Ruby...but he assures me that it is over between them. Aunt Jer and Uncle Homi feel it has been over a long time ago, but just not finalized."

Hearing this, her mother jumped up from the table as if someone has thrown a glass of icy cold water at her. Throwing her napkin down in angry frustration she said through gritted teeth...

"Ava! you know this is no time to indulge in company that is problematic... One whiff of scandal and all our efforts to find you a suitable partner will be ruined. You do understand that don't you?" She seemed panicked at what she had just heard.

Shaking her head with profound disapproval, she said, "I am surprised that Jer and Homi have said nothing about this.... I shall have a talk with them. Ava, you wanted my advice so I am giving it to you clearly... you are not to see this man again... under any circumstances... do you understand, do you understand?" she emphasized, her flushed face hovering inches over Ava's.

Ava felt like someone had just slapped her. The earlier euphoria she had felt coming into the Sea Lounge evaporated into a well of disappointment. She seemed to have unintentionally painted herself into a corner, being forbidden both by her mother and her own conscience, to see Adil again. She had made the decision and the decision had been made for her. Ruby's presence even in her absence was being felt and respected.

Chapter 20
Adil and Mithu

Ava thought she was dreaming when she heard the familiar beep, beep of Adil's car. Its way too early she thought and pulled the pillow over her head, as if that would block her longing for Adil.

Beep, beep, she heard it again despite the pillow over her ears. She jumped out of bed and ran to one of many windows that overlooked the street. He saw her, looked up at her with love, waved and smiled holding the sight of her and not wanting to look away. Ava pointed to her nightgown and her disheveled hair.

He mouthed the words, "Take your time, I will wait."

Ava did a jig of pleasure around her bedroom. Racing to shower and dress, she threw all thoughts of caution to the wind.

Aunt Jer had just woken up like clockwork at 7am and was having her first cup of tea and wondered if that really could be the beep-beep of Adil's car this early in the morning. Her thoughts were answered as Ava came rushing into the dining room, bursting with news that Adil was downstairs waiting for her. Aunt Jer sighed, not knowing whether to be relieved or worried.

"Ava have a cup of tea; I have put lemongrass and mint in the teapot." But Ava had to run downstairs. "Everything is a rush with the younger generation," Jer thought, throwing up her hands in acceptance.

She was amazed at the change in her niece. Gone were the dark circles under her eyes, the pained look she had worn these past days as if someone had killed her firstborn. Ava balanced from one foot to the other in excited impatience. She felt famished. Glowing with excited anticipation of meeting Adil, Ava took two large bites of toast, two large gulps of fragrant tea, kissed her aunt and sailed down the stairs.

Adil had parked his car, crossed the street and entered the threshold of the building, waiting for her at the foot of the stairs.

She was walking on air. Halfway down the last flight of stairs, she suddenly froze. Adil's eyes questioned as she seemed to turn pale.

Ava had suddenly remembered...

"Adil I will not be able to go with you..." she said slowly but firmly.

"Ava why?" he asked in anguish.

She gazed at him, their eyes locked and holding, neither showing any desire to break away. Their hearts playing tug of war.

"Ruby," Ava said flatly. Her insides twisting... struggling to gain control of her composure.

"It is being resolved Ava; she is preparing to move to Australia as we speak... but I respect your reservations."

Their hands stretched along the diagonal of the banister instinctively intertwining fingers, waves of raw emotion coursing through them. Her hands as silky as a dove's wing, his were a firm trapeze artist's grip. She finally pulled away trembling, tears threatening to spill but kept at bay by her strong will.

He turned away, dejected and dazed as he made his way to the car.

Sita, the pavement dweller, who was a single mother with a baby, had been preoccupied for a few seconds and taken her eyes of little Mithu, who had crawled to the edge of the pavement making his way onto the road. Adil's car brakes screeched to a halt. Jumping out of the car shocked at almost running over the child, he impulsively scooped up Mithu looking around for his mother. Sita turned around at the sound of the cars brakes and realizing Mithu had escaped her vigilance screamed and ran to retrieve him.

"Sorry, sorry *Sahib*, I thought baby was still sleeping. He has just started crawling and has become so fast. Sorry, *Sahib*."

Adil was not listening to Sita's apologies. His relief at avoiding a tragedy was palpable. When his heartbeat came back to normal his attention was drawn to Mithu's cleft lip.

"Is this a problem for you?" he pointed to the cleft lip, still holding Mithu who was gurgling and grabbing at his sunglasses, with the innocent playfulness of a child.

"He has no future with that disfiguration," Sita said, eyes downcast, face flushed, resigned to the situation.

She reached to take Mithu from Adil's arms but Mithu screamed indignation.

Adil opened the door to his car started the engine and sat in a trance thinking about the drama that had just unfolded before him and the yawning emptiness he felt without Ava. Just holding her hand had filled him with strength and hope, however faint, of a promising future filled with deep contentment.

Mithu was still crying and holding out his hands towards Adil.

In that moment Adil made a decision. He got out of the car and walked over to Sita.

She drew back afraid as his shadow fell over her.

"Please don't be afraid, I think I can help your son..."

His earnest demeanor cautiously relaxed Sita who was pulling her saree over her head almost covering her whole face, as if to shield herself.

"I have a doctor friend who can fix your child's lip."

Still wary but curious at this stranger offering to help her, she listened.

"If you agree, go and see this doctor" he said scribbling a name and address on the back of his business card.

"But *Sahib*, I cannot afford it!" she said.

He raised his hand in assurance, "I will be paying for it. Namaste."

"Namaste," she said. The pavement dweller and the benefactor bowed to each other, both carrying their own personal burden.

He drove off wondering how he was going to gain Ava's trust without being given the opportunity to spend time with her.

Ava had been watching the scene unfold and had stifled a scream at the baby's narrow escape from the wheels of Adil's car. She felt she was partly to blame because Adil was so upset and preoccupied after her sudden rejection of him.

The next day, while Jer and Homi were taking their after-lunch nap, Ava quietly unlatched the front door and went downstairs and across to Mithu's mother Sita.

"What happened yesterday, Sita?" she asked.

"*Memsahib*, I do not know what to do anymore. I cannot work because Mithu is now too grown up to be left alone and I need to buy milk to feed him."

"I will give you money for his milk as long as my aunt does not see me, so do not let that worry you for now."

"You are very kind *Memsahib* and yesterday *Sahib* saved my son and also gave me the name of a doctor who could fix Mithu's mouth."

Sita showed Ava, Adil's business card with the doctor's name and details scribbled on the back of it.

Ava's heart melted. She knew Adil could have easily just given Sita a few pennies to placate her or even driven off in a huff, but he did not. On the contrary he had decided to be a Good Samaritan and do the utmost for Sita and Mithu. As Untouchables, they were unlikely to ever get help from anyone. Her instincts about Adil's integrity were confirmed.

The next day when Adil phoned she accepted his invitation.

Chapter 21
Love Letters on Leaves

After the wonderful surprises the Bombay countryside had offered them, Ava and Adil wanted to go back and explore more places, never knowing what pleasant surprises awaited them.

Ava felt like a bouncing ball of sunshine, driving through the Bombay countryside beside Adil, their fingers and hearts entwined. The light drizzle had faded and a bright hot sun came out to meet the lush green meadows and carpets of wild flowers.

"Where are we heading Ava?"

"I'll know the place to stop, when I see it," she said with a mischievous laugh, winding down the window and enjoying the breeze blow through her hair.

Ever obliging, Adil put his new Ambassador car into fourth gear and let it purr along, Ava snuggled up beside him.

Carefree and elated to be together, breathing in fresh post-monsoon air, life felt as light and airy as their surroundings.

They turned off a country road and stopped at the end of it, totally entranced by the majestic sight before them.

A huge waterfall cascaded down, the thundering water cooling the warm rocks and sending sprays of steam hissing upward in a cloud. The lush greenery fed by the waterfall looked fresh and inviting. Green ferns nodded in the spray, thick and luxurious. Ava looked at Adil, found him smiling, and knew they had discovered another of nature's miracles.

Lifting her skirt, and throwing off her sandals, Ava dipped her toes in the tempting water, only to find it too freezing cold to swim in. She bent over and splashed some of the fresh water on her face, neck and throat and then lay down on a warm flat rock, taking in a deep breath of bliss as she had never known it before. She knew she would always remember this place and all the emotions that it had stirred up with its pristine beauty. And of course, with Adil by her side.

Adil had his head on her stomach, hearing her heartbeat. When Ava stroked his face and playfully rumpled his hair, her gentle loving touch was like magic, touching the depths of his soul. Blissful hours passed by quicker than they would have wished for.

The sun had set, showing off its brilliant colors of orange, bright yellow with streaks of lavender and pink.

Adil gazed at Ava, her hair spread all around her beautiful face. Her nipples were erect and visible through her cotton blouse. He longed to tear off her blouse and make passionate love to her, but he knew he had to restrain himself till they were married.

The monsoon rain had cleaned away the dust of summer. The trees looked freshly washed. Flowers showed their appreciation, blooming and waving in the breeze. A kaleidoscope of blossoms in colors and fragrances, as far as the eye could see, intoxicated and delighted their senses.

"Seems we have found our spot!" Ava said, "What do you think Adil?"

He answered with a happy smile and hugged her close.

Spreading a large cloth under a tree that generously offered shade, they unpacked their picnic basket. Sandwiches and cold beer had never tasted so good they both agreed, with a kiss that sent their senses clamoring for more. There was no one around them and after the frenzied jostling of people in the city, the countryside offered a cool, leisurely respite.

A clutch of pigeons had come strutting over to pick at the remains of their picnic and cooed and ruffled their feathers contentedly, showing no signs of being in a hurry to fly away.

With Adil's arm around Ava's shoulders, they strolled through the fabulous bounty of flowers and shrubs, feeling the soothing green grass under their bare feet. Adil plucked a bunch of fragrant Champa (fragrant flower) and gallantly presented it to Ava with a flourish and a bow.

Leisurely admiring the natural beauty before them, they spotted the spectacular Peacock Tree filled with the sound of birdsong and its large heart-shaped leaves.

"I am going to write you love letters on these leaves, till you beg me to stop," teased Adil.

Ava smiled, suddenly feeling a blush work its way from her throat to her cheeks. She asked, shyly, "May I write one to you?"

Adil saw her blush and looked away as if that would hide her sudden shyness.

He said simply, "I would cherish your love letters forever."

For the next half hour there was silence, smiles and furrowed brows, as each concentrated on putting their thoughts and feelings on the heart-shaped leaves.

On one leaf Adil drew a circle and wrote, "My love for you is unconditional and forever."

On another he wrote, "My happiness begins and ends with your love." On yet another he wrote, "If we are ever parted I will search the world for you."

On the last one, he wrote in his beautiful handwriting, one word that he felt said it all, "FOREVER."

Ava, dressed in a white silk blouse with cap sleeves and a jean skirt, was lying on her stomach, deep in thought, chewing the end of her pen, her long golden legs folded up in an L shape. After writing several "letters" she decided her favorite would be one word. She wrote in large print on a perfect peacock tree leaf, "FOREVER."

Ava looked over at him and said "No peeking, Adil."

He smiled. "I don't have to peek, my love; my pen seems to know what my heart and soul already know."

On the last leaf Ava wrote, "You are the beginning of my everything."

They had kept their love letters on leaves to themselves, planning to share them later, when they had to say goodbye.

Sunbeams spilled through the branches of the peacock tree drawing intricate designs on Ava's long, magnificent hair, outlining her fine features. There was an ethereal, delicate sweetness to her that mesmerized Adil. He propped himself up on one hand, admiring the flowing lines of her body, feeling overcome with how fortunate he was in having found her. Never had he known an affection so healing, sincere, pure and profound. Ava had revived his spirit and faith in the future. He knew he could never live happily without her. She looked so fragile, vulnerable and trusting, he resolved to do everything he could to shield her from harm, and be deserving of her trust.

The sunset was divine and Ava thought, God had the best artists working for Him, creating the most breathtaking works of art in nature. The bright sheath of light across the horizon that heralds the majestic sunset, was their cue that it was time to start for home. Returning their picnic basket to the car's trunk, they took one last long look at the serenity around them. They kissed and held each other as misty-eyed young lovers do.

Adil cranked the Ambassador into gear and slowly drove back into the city. Ava pressed the flowers Adil had thoughtfully picked for her against her cheeks. The car was filled with the heady fragrance of the flowers, reminders of a memorable happy day that would be etched in their memories forever. With her head on Adil's shoulder, she wished this idyllic day would never end and that they could peacefully marry, with their family's blessings.

"Ava, when shall I meet your parents?" Adil asked, mirroring her thoughts.

"Soon," Ava said, a shiver going through her as she drew closer to him.

They had arrived at Gowalia Tank and could see that the pavement dwellers were already fast asleep on their straw mats, blankets wrapped around themselves like parcels.

Particularly reticent to part that evening, they said goodbye several times, choosing one love letter to exchange. Neither could bring themselves to leave.

From the many "letters on leaves" they had written to each other, they both decided, *unbeknownst to the other*, that they would exchange the one that said "FOREVER."

At last, seeing Aunty Jer anxiously peering from the window, Ava tore herself away from Adil, and tarried awhile on the stairs.

They blew each other kisses until she disappeared from view.

Chapter 22
Ava and Adil Meet her Parents

Adil had suggested that he meet and answer all the questions that Ava's family had for him. Though reluctant, Ava's parents had agreed to gather at Jer's flat and meet the young man, face to face.

Jer, Homi, Ava and her parents Dina and Darius, sat stone- faced and apart from each other, as if the subject they were going to be discussing was contagious. An unpleasantness hung in the air.

Everyone was on edge and busy with their thoughts as the doorbell rang, at exactly 2pm jangling their already skittish nerves.

Jer jumped up and darted to the door as if catapulted there, ushering in Adil with a tepid smile.

Everyone stood up to meet Adil as he greeted them with warm handshakes. He looked clean-shaven, fresh, fit, muscular and at least a head taller than everyone else. He had an open, eager demeanor about him.

Ava's father Darius, cleared his throat a few times and spoke.
"Well, young man, I hear you have intentions of marrying my daughter Ava?"
"Yes, Mr. Darius Byramji, with your and Mrs. Byramji's blessings, that is my respectful intention."
"Well, Mr. Adil Irani, we do not know anything about yourself or your family. We would have liked your parents or a representative of

your family to be present here today," Darius said in an authoritative voice.

"Mr. Darius, I thought Ava may have mentioned that my parents have passed on and my elder brother Rusi was not invited to join us today. Perhaps a future meeting with him can be planned?"

"Ava has not informed us of your brother Rusi and I am saddened to hear your parents are not alive," he said, his tone softening.

"What is your background, Mr. Irani? How do you meet the requirements of an eligible partner to Ava?" Darius asked.

"Please call me Adil," he paused, and then said, "Mr. Darius your daughter has changed my life for the better and in return for her love, I promise to strive with all within my power to ensure she is always happy and well-cared for..."

"That is a lofty promise to make Adil, can you back that up with facts?"

Ava gripped Jer's arm tightly.

"I am a businessman Mr. Darius, mine is a rags to riches background, with no inheritance to my name. I have managed to prosper and can offer Ava a comfortable lifestyle," said Adil humbly.

Darius coughed, "Ava has expensive tastes, Adil. I fear you will not be able to meet her needs on the juice stores, I am told, you own."

"I beg to differ, Mr. Darius. I also own my own flat and car and I am planning to expand my business, which I am sure you would approve of..." said Adil confidently.

"Hmmm, I somehow doubt what you can offer Ava is able to meet our expectations as a partner for her," he paused.

"You see we would only consider a doctor as a husband for her thereby assuring her needs and wants will be met... it's also more prestigious than a businessman with two juice shops. No insult meant Adil. I am sure you understand as a father I want the best for my daughter... she is rather special!"

"I will agree with you that she is indeed very special. As far as being a doctor, that I am not, but... if that is the requirement to seal this deal then I have a proposition!"

Dina spoke quickly before Darius could answer, hope in her voice. "What is your proposition, Adil?"

Jer, Homi and Ava were on the edge of their sofas leaning forward tense and taut.

Ava's father cleared his throat a few times and then haughtily raised his head and asked, "What is this proposition you have that can possibly sway us into believing you are worthy of marrying my daughter?"

"Mr. Darius Byramji, I have completed my Bachelor of Science degree and I am willing to attend medical school and train to be a doctor, if that is what it will take for me to have Ava's hand in marriage!"

There was a collective gasp. Homi went white with shock. Jer clapped her hands over her open mouth and Dina turned away with a thoughtful smile hidden behind the back of her hand against her mouth. She was dumbfounded at Adil's chutzpah. She could not believe he was able to go toe to toe with her domineering husband.

Ava bit on her white-knuckles till there were teeth marks.

Darius looked at Adil for the first time as a possible worthy adversary. The room that minutes ago had been filled with apprehension, now had pin drop silence at Adil's response to Ava's father.

"It is a far-fetched proposition Adil, but I thank you for trying to meet our requirements for Ava, you have put forth a noble proposition and I hope you find yourself a loving wife... unfortunately we cannot agree to give you our Ava's hand in marriage."

Ava's knees buckled as she quietly slid to the floor in a faint. Everyone began to frantically fan her with whatever was nearby... a newspaper, a cushion. Ava's mother gave her father dagger looks as she gently swabbed Ava's face and neck with a cold compress that Jer had handed her.

Adil was on his knees at Ava's side feeling deeply concerned and guilty, wondering whether he was responsible for Ava's fainting spell. He had not previously discussed studying to be a doctor with Ava. Hearing her father insist that it was a prerequisite for them to accept him as a viable husband had compelled him to make an instantaneous decision with the full intention of going through with that proposition.

He felt deflated and defeated at the fact that he had been unsuccessful in winning over Ava's father. He felt for a moment there was a spark of approval from her mother, who seemed to be considering his proposition.

With Ava revived, everyone's focus shifted to Darius. He answered their questioning looks with a silent and hasty exit. Running to keep up with him was a frustrated Dina who wanted to voice her opinion but was silenced with one look at her husband's face, which had returned to its stony demeanor.

Chapter 23
Raju's Training

Waking up with the dawn, Anand, the leader of the group of boys filled a bucket of water to the brim. He swore as he lugged it from the park to the dirty corner of the street the boys called home.

He said to Raju, "Raju, this will be your training today, while we are gone. You cannot go on the streets until you are properly trained, otherwise you could get us all into trouble with the police, understand?"

Raju nodded his sleepy head in agreement, longing for the training to be over so he could go into action with the boys.

"There is a coin at the bottom of this bucket of water. Your training today is to try and get the coin out of the water without making even a ripple in the water, do you understand?" Anand asked, while the other boys grinned and laughed at the new trainee.

"Is that all I have to do all day?" asked Raju, thinking this had to be a joke they were playing on him.

"It seems easier than it looks. Keep practicing until you can show me you can easily retrieve that coin from the bottom of the bucket, without making a ripple in the water, okay?" Anand said, looking stern.

The boys were now all awake and went to make their morning ablutions in the park, washing as best they could under the drip of a single faucet. Then they went to the chaiwala's[12] rickety wood shack for a breakfast of hot sweet tea.

When they had dispersed, leaving Raju alone, he tried to practice the task Anand had ordered him to repeat, till he was able to master it. He tried, repeating it over and over again but could not get that darn coin without disturbing the water.

Soon it was noon and scorching hot. He decided to take a little nap and try again later.

He awoke as the sun was setting, to the boys gently kicking him.

"You are going to starve if you think you can sleep and make money," Anand snapped. "Do you want to be a lazy *ladoo*[13] or be an expert pickpocket earning lots of rupees?"

"I want to be an expert pickpocket and earn lots of rupees," Raju replied with conviction.

"If you mean that, you must keep trying till you show me you can do it. If you succeed you can have food. If you do not you get only scraps or go hungry till you learn."

Seeing Anand's steely demeanor, the other boys tried not to snicker. Sitting cross-legged, they ate hungrily, taking handfuls of rice and curry from a banana leaf to their mouths.

Raju's stomach growled with hunger and he longed to stop trying to get that coin from the bottom of the bucket. He knew he had to persevere. Going hungry again was not an option. Flattening his hand, he used his fingers with utmost sensitivity and got the coin without disturbing the water.

"*Shabash!*[14]" Anand congratulated him, saying. "Now go eat, your food is wrapped in the banana leaf near your blanket. We are going to sleep and I suggest you do the same. Tomorrow will be another day of training."

Within minutes, the boys dropped off to sleep, while Raju hungrily ate large handfuls of rice and potato curry that the boys had bought for him. He washed his hands in the park and lying on his

---

[12] tea vendor's
[13] round sweetmeat
[14] well done!

blanket, his hand under his head for a pillow, gazed at the millions of stars wondering what tomorrow would bring.

He slept. A rat bit his toe that night, but it did not awaken him. He only realized in the morning that he had a bloody toe, and swore at the rat that had long disappeared. It would eventually heal, he thought, limping to his next task as he tried to put it out of his mind. These things were expected when you lived on Bombay's filthy streets. Soon he would be rich and no rat would be able to get near him.

He smiled at the thought as he set about his second exercise.

Anand had bought a melon and covered it with a thin gauzy fabric. Handing Raju, a razor blade, he instructed him to cut through the fabric without grazing the skin of the melon.

The boys lost themselves in the jam-packed streets like invisible ghosts. Raju was alone again under the merciless blistering hot sun. Sweat poured down his face, armpits and back. He cut through the cloth over and over again, scoring the melon's skin every which way. He was hot, tired and very tempted to eat the cool melon. But Anand's words rang in his ears and he knew this would be his only chance at honing his skills to the level of the other boys. He must persevere.

Getting up from his squatting position he headed to the only cool place in his surroundings, the tap of running water in the park. Luckily there was no line up, so he opened the tap and let the cold water soak him completely.

As the water ran down his head, face, back and arms, he felt re-energized and his flagging spirits rose. Returning to the sorry sight of the melon covered in the cloth with scores of cuts, still dripping wet, he sat cross-legged, pulled the cloth covered melon towards him, took the razor and concentrated on the task at hand. With an agile sensitivity, he managed to cut through the cloth without a scratch on the melon's skin. Cautiously optimistic he repeated his new found skill until the cloth was ripped and a good portion of the melon's skin was untouched.

He did not have long to wait before the sun finally set and the boys returned. After a long day running through crowds with the sun ceaselessly beating down on them, they returned tired, hot, dusty and hungry. They lined up at the tap for its cold comfort, soon joining Raju who could hardly wait to demonstrate what he hoped he had mastered.

Anand recognized the gleam in Raju's eyes and the way in which he seemed to want his attention. Kicking him gently, Anand said with an air of bravado, "So have you lazed around all day, or have you taught yourself something useful? We can't keep feeding lazy ladoos like you, for nothing, eh, understand?"

Raju nervously asked, "Can I show you what I've practiced?"
With all the boys and Anand sitting cross-legged in a circle he took the razor, focused, and repeatedly cut through the cloth without grazing the melon. The boys laughed and good-naturedly slapped him on the back of his head.

"Now, you are one of us and can earn rupees. Tomorrow you will come with me, don't get too cocky or you will land us all in the hands of the police. We bought you rice and potato curry, so let us eat. Tomorrow I will show this green banana how to be an expert pickpocket," Anand jokingly pointed a finger at Raju, "so he can buy us some rice and curry for a change."

Anand seemed proud of his protégé and Raju felt like he had finally joined a family. They all laughed, a happy den of thieves, complicit in their common goal.

After the boys wolfed down their meal, they sat around discussing possible areas of the city for Raju and Anand to tackle the next day.

Yawning and stretching, their bellies filled with food, they lay on their blankets and fell into a deep, satisfied sleep.

The next morning, Raju woke up early, washed at the tap and eagerly awaited the other boys. Anand gave half a smile when he saw Raju ready to go. He sighed and hoped this rookie would not get them into trouble.

He felt Raju at the tender age of seven was a brave boy with a lot of promise. After all he had passed his rigorous training in record time. He did not let on that it had taken him many frustrating weeks to master what Raju had done in just two days.

They crowded around the tea shack, slurping tea, from which steam rose in wisps. Then they dispersed, leaving Anand and Raju alone.

Anand said, "I've decided. We will go to the Tardeo area. It is close to Gowalia Tank."

Anand told Raju that he should make eye contact with him, before tackling anyone. He suggested that for the first few pickpocketing's he should just give the person a light shove, before relieving them of their wallet. The shove would not be noticed in the crush of jostling crowds of people, hurrying to work or shopping. The streets were always densely crowded and that suited Anand well.

Coming toward them was a man wearing the colorful clothes of a tourist, camera slung over his neck. As he took a photo of the Tardeo circle, Raju told Anand he would try this one.

He nodded to Raju giving him the go ahead. Tourists were an ideal mark for beginners. Keeping with the rhythmic strides of the masses on the street, Raju deftly slid his hand into the man's right pant pocket where he had seen a slight bulge, felt his hand close around the wallet. He slid it out and quickly zig-zagged away into the crowd.

By the time the tourist had gotten his photo, his wallet was far away. Anand kept his eye on Raju, proudly watching him weave in and out of the crowds, choosing his targets with an uncanny instinctiveness for relieving them of their rupees.

After the third pickpocket of the day, Raju was elated, a bit nervous and tired. He signaled Anand that he was heading "home," and ran ahead with the wallet and other cash hidden on his small body.

Finally, he reached the corner of the park that they called home, perspiring heavily and bent over almost out of breath. He was tempted to go to the tap for its cooling promise, but he pushed the thought aside and instead carefully looked around at his surroundings, before he unloaded his precious loot, hiding it under his blanket and pushing it all further behind the palm tree there.

Still nervous and despite being very hot and thirsty, he patiently awaited the arrival of the other boys, before he finally went and sat under the tap and let its cold magic quench his thirst and cool his overheated body.

The boys were excited, chattering with Anand about how well Raju had done. They all thumped him on the back. Well after sunset, the group took out the loot they had collected that day. To their surprise, Raju had the most rupees. They teased and elbowed him good naturedly as they sat in a circle, cross-legged, and opened their banana leaves for dinner.

Anand grinned. "Hey Raju, tomorrow you buy us food and sweetmeats and maybe go to the temple!"

The next day Raju did just that. Placing the fruit, incense and sweetmeats in front of the deities at the temple his quivering hand belied his unease and questioning of the morality of his way of life.

Contrite and afraid of the stone-faced deities that he faced; he repeatedly rang the temple bell feeling it would expunge the shame he felt. Praying for forgiveness he promised God he would do some good, later in his life. In the meantime, he pleaded for acceptance of robbing rich men for sheer survival.

A crack of thunder whipped across the sky; a swift wind arose suddenly clanging the temple door shut. Raju the big, strong, sinewy thug, legs turning to jelly, scared out of his wits, jumped up, ran to open the heavy doors and escape into the streets.

For a few long minutes the thug had reverted to the scrawny insecure seven-year-old boy. With a guilty conscience he cut his day short and went home in a contemplative mood, deciding on treating the boys to the movies. They loved Bollywood films and idolized the film stars. Bingeing on the movies, transported them to the lavish lifestyles of the rich and famous and lovers caught in a tangle, with an eventual happy resolution.

They returned to their blankets in the park, robustly singing movie songs and imitating the dance moves they had just seen.

Raju picked at his teeth, accepting that pickpocketing and movies had helped him survive the mean, filthy streets of Bombay.

It was the law of the jungle. Children had to quickly become adults or be left begging or dead, he reasoned.

By the time Raju turned 18 he was an expert that trained other pickpockets and charged them for the training. Lithe and strong, he had also become a thug for hire. His price was high— his preferred tool a steel pipe. If the price was right, he would do the job and do it well. He knew how much force to use to scare someone into submission. Business was brisk as he treated each job seriously and with the same intense diligence he had applied to his pickpocketing training.

One thing rankled all of them. Through all the years, despite their combined earnings they could not find suitable accommodation in this space-starved city. Moving to a shanty town meant moving away from the city and surrounding areas which were the main source of their income. Still, it seemed like their only option.

After repeatedly being tossed out of the park by the police who yelled that sleeping there was not allowed, Raju decided to look for an alternative place. The gang needed a safe place to rest after long, sweaty days on the streets.

Their only alternative was to ride the train to the outskirts of the city each evening. There, they had built a rough shelter from bits of tin and cardboard, covering it all with sheets of plastic stolen from an unguarded construction site and laboriously carrying bricks from the same site to their newly erected shelter to anchor the plastic sheeting in place.

This was the best they had ever lived and though it took longer to get home each day, Raju and the boys felt a stronger sense of togetherness. Some nights if they did not get to the train in time or were caught by the train conductor for riding on top of the train, they stayed in the city and endured whatever the weather brought with it. Hardened by the rigors of living on the pavement and the park, the boys took everything in their stride.

In the darkness of midnight, Raju was shaken awake by a stealthy figure. Disturbed, the boys grumbled and rolled over in their sleep.

"What is it?" Raju asked in a sleepy voice.

"*Memsahib* Ruby has a job for you."

He was instructed where and when to meet her for further details. Before Raju could ask for more information, the messenger had blended into the shadows of the night.

Chapter 24
Ruby's Games

Ruby's flight from New York to Bombay, touched down on time. Ruby gave Adil an offhand kiss on the cheek, silent tension simmering between them.

He stared straight ahead of him and said, "Ruby when you have rested, we need to have a serious talk about the future."
"Oh Lord! The future, the future! Is that all you can think about!" Ruby said shaking her head and giving him a sideways look of exasperation. She turned her back to him, sticking her tongue out.

The status quo suited Ruby perfectly and she had no plans to make any changes. Adil could go on bleating about marriage and "Their future" if he wanted, but she was comfortable with things just the way they were, and that was all that mattered, she thought, smiling knowingly to herself.
"Adil you are being tiresome with this talk about the future. I will discuss this with you when we get home."

Later, refreshed after having a long nap and a bubble bath, she sauntered into the living room wearing one of his long cotton t-shirts.
Finding him pacing up and down, she asked nonchalantly, "Adil, what is on your mind?" She yawned expecting a version of the usual subject "When are we going to get married and settle down!"

Damn the man, she thought. Why could he not just let sleeping dogs lie, life was ideal just the way it was.

Nothing had prepared Ruby for the bombshell news from Adil.

Adil drew up a chair opposite Ruby and looked her in the eye.

"Ruby, I have met a young lady that I wish to marry!"

Her Adil with someone else?

"What are you ranting about Adil, who is this tramp that you suddenly want to marry?" she said, spitting out the words.

For once in her shrewdly planned life, Ruby was thrown for a loop. She had not seen this development coming, and her natural impulse was to fight any inconvenience to her.

If she had to pick "mean" "nasty" and "ruthless" from her toolbox that is what she would choose.

"What has gotten into you Adil?" she asked. "You know I will not allow that to happen! Who is this tart you suddenly want and what has been going on while I have been away?" She asked in rapid fire questions, throwing her coffee cup at him.

He managed to duck in time, weary at this habit of hers whenever they had a disagreement.

"She is no tart, Ruby. I met Ava Byramji at Eruch's party and have found in her all I have ever hoped for. Anyway, I do not want to discuss her with you."

She flung her saucer at him and it went whizzing through the air, missing him and crashing to the floor. He saw her walk into the kitchen and return with a pile of dinner plates, which she placed on the table.

Adil remained calm but firm "Ruby, I want you to move out."

Hearing this, Ruby changed her response. Removing the t-shirt, she was wearing, she let it slip to the floor and sat on Adil's lap. She put her arm around his neck, naked except for her sandals balancing on her toes.

"Adil darling I am going to settle in Sydney, Australia and I have managed to get a visa for you." She said with her face close to his neck.

"We could open a business there and prosper together. Can you see what a great opportunity this is for us?"

"Ruby, please put your clothes on. I am not interested in going to Sydney or anywhere else with you," Adil replied, pushing her off his lap. He was weary of her trying to resolve issues by seduction.

"Please Ruby, you know there has been no love between us for years, let's part amicably," Adil said, trying to reason with her.

"I will move you out of this flat and into a luxury suite at the Taj Hotel which I will pay for, until it's time for you to leave for Sydney. Ruby, its high time for us both to be comfortable and move to a place of real happiness."

Ruby was not moved. With a swipe of her hand, she sent the remaining dishes from the table cascading to the floor.

"I'm tired of these outbursts, Ruby. Can't we rationally discuss matters?" Adil said, annoyed at the broken glass strewn all over the living room floor.

"Ruby, you do not seem to care about the scandal you have caused by moving in. You know it is not the done thing here in Bombay. It's not like we are living in Europe or the USA!"

She was aware she had caused a scandal and maligned his reputation by moving into his flat.

Angrily aiming her sandal at him she cried, "Like I care!"

"You never really wanted to marry me, did you?" Adil said quietly.

She answered him by removing her other sandal and throwing it at him.

Ruby was furious. She had plans in which Adil played a crucial role. Knowing that Adil wanted to part as quickly and uneventfully as possible did not suit her. She would have to find another way to keep Adil on her leash. Usually, her throwing a tantrum would result in

Adil, however reluctantly, give in to her wishes. He did so not from a lack of courage, but simply to avoid the drama of broken plates and things being thrown around.

However, today, he had stood stoically impassive.

Was she losing him?

She decided to change her approach and give him the idea that she was coming around to the idea of leaving the flat without making a scene.

Ruby admired her freshly manicured bright red nails. These hands were not meant to bother with running a business in Sydney or anywhere else. She had better things to do than work, she thought to herself. That job belonged to Adil and she needed him to work retail hours, run the business for them and handle whatever problems presented themselves. Adil was going to be her designated work horse, she had decided.

She needed free time to flirt and enjoy a life of leisure. She was damned if that bitch Ava was going to spoil her grand plan.

Pretending to make reservations to go to Sydney by herself, she asked Adil to drive her around, so that she could prepare to leave. Every day she had a request to be driven somewhere in preparation for her new life in Sydney. She would take hours at the travel agency and then the next day the same would happen at the currency exchange. Of course, she needed to buy sarees and then there was the tailor and the umpteen fittings she needed for her saree blouses.

To keep the peace and with hope that Ruby would go peacefully, Adil agreed to drive her around to her many appointments and patiently waited for her to emerge from each one.

By the time she completed each errand, she knew it would be too late for Adil to see Ava. She kept Adil busy driving her to the travel agent and other places she insisted were necessary in her preparation for her life in Australia.

This ruse had managed to keep Adil away from Ava for three whole days, and had given Ruby a sense of victory.

Her immediate plan was to keep Adil away from Ava for as long as possible. So far it had worked, and she planned to extend it if she could. Anyway, he had no business in being interested in a little South African girl when he could have her, she thought. He would soon come to his senses and see that Ava was just a mirage, and Ruby was the only real deal, she reckoned.

Chapter 25
Eruch's Promise

Ruby woke up with a mission on her mind. First, she was going to visit Eruch, the Immigration Officer charmed by her. For him, she would make his favorite Rum Pudding. She looked through her wardrobe and decided on a clingy black jersey dress with a plunging neckline.

As the afternoon cooled, she asked Adil to take her to Eruch's office to drop off the Rum Pudding. Adil wanting to avoid an argument, drove her to the Immigration Office building.

"Adil would you be a darling and wait for me, I promise not to be long?"

Ruby made her grand entrance into Eruch's office. After presenting the Rum Pudding with an extravagant flourish, she drew closer, lightly brushing off non-existent fluff from his starched white shirt.

"Eruch darling, would you like to do me a favor?" she asked in a slow, syrupy, seductive drawl, making sure he was noticing her breasts.

"Of course, of course Ruby, what is it?"

"I want you *not* to sign off on Ava Byramji's passport until the day after Adil and I are married!" she said curling her lips with satisfaction.

"But Ruby I always sign off the passports of the Byramji family," he sputtered. "I have been doing it on every visit. Darius Byramji is my long-time friend!"

Her request surprised Eruch. Ruby had never wanted to marry Adil. She had always told him he was just a *convenience*. So why this sudden rush to marry him and what had Ava to do with it?

Ruby explained in a rather flustered tone that Adil had apparently fallen in love with Ava and they planned to marry very soon. She needed Eruch's help to see that did not happen.

"Is this Adil and Ava thing really serious?" he asked dubiously, "I have never seen him even flirt with anyone... you have been away so often on trips, he could have..."

Before Eruch had the opportunity to get an answer from her, Ruby had put her face an inch away from his with a full view of her heaving breasts and asked with her usual guile, "Well, will you promise to do this for me, darling Eruch?

"For you darling Ruby, I will promise anything you ask," Eruch said, like a dog with its tongue hanging out and tail wagging, eager to please its master.

Ruby brushed her breast against his cheek and left the office with a smug smile.

So, the first part of her plan was in place. Ava would be stuck in the country until and unless Adil married her and subsequently became her work horse in Sydney, Australia. She was pleased with herself.

Now for the second part of her plan, she had to find her hoodlum friend Raju. As she stepped into the idling car with Adil patiently waiting, her mind was whirring. She had to find Raju and that was not always easy. He seemed to have this chameleon like ability to make himself disappear.

Chapter 26
The Attack

Adil had parked the car around the corner from Jer's building. After the exquisite day in the country, he and Ava had lingered awhile in the car. Finally, Adil got out of the car and escorted Ava to the building.

Ava had an uneasy feeling, as though someone was following them. She mentioned this to Adil, but he laughed, brushing aside her fear, saying, "In Bombay you have to expect someone would always be walking behind or around you."

She heard footsteps in time with theirs and turning around instinctively, saw something long and silver. The next thing she knew was Adil was being knocked to the pavement by a man with frightening, bloodshot eyes and a fight ensued. Her hands raised to her mouth, she screamed as she saw the man stab Adil in the ribs.

Adil's bodybuilding chops helped him swiftly take the man down, rip the knife out of his hand, punch him in the face, putting a choke hold on him. Blood was dripping from a deep gash on Adil's hand and chest area, but he did not care. He was livid with anger.

"Who sent you, tell me who sent you and why you attacked me?" Adil shouted, getting ready to tighten his choke hold on the attacker. Adil would not let him go and told Ava in a firm tone to go upstairs and be safe in Aunt Jer's flat. Adil was hurt and she hesitated in leaving him, but he was angry and adamant in his demand of her. She reluctantly agreed.

Before she could leave, Lungri, the one-legged pavement dweller, never one to miss a fight, came hobbling over on her crutch, wanting to know what was going on. Before she could say a word, shock registered on her face!

Lungri's mouth was wide open in horror! She was staring in disbelief at the person in the choke hold.

"Raju, is that you? Raju answer me," she demanded.

"I have not seen you since you ran away at the age of seven... when I found money on my blanket, I knew only you would have left it for me, I felt proud that you were doing well in your life."

She paused, pulling her saree over her face, deeply embarrassed at her son's actions.

"I named you after a king, hoping that you would get educated and take us off the pavement. It seems like you have become a king of thugs!"

She spat at him, fury and intense pain in her eyes and continued, "This woman Ava has been extremely kind and respectful to all of us pavement dwellers. I am ashamed and angry beyond words, that a son of mine brought up with so much love, has now become a thug, who earns his living by hurting people.

"Who paid you? I demand you tell the *sahib* you hit, who it is who paid you!"

The choke hold on Raju was getting tighter. Blood was staining Adil's shirt and pants. He tightened the hold.

"Tell me who sent you and I will not harm you or call the police."

The thug's hands flailing around indicated he was accepting his loss. Raju finally blurted out, "*Memsahib* Ruby!"

Adil let him go and Raju ran off expertly blending into the night, relieved that the police had not been called.

"Why did you let him go, you have lost a lot of blood, may I get a taxi to take you to the hospital?" Lungri asked, alarmed and distressed.

Adil replied, "Lungri, I let him go because I did not want to cause *you* more pain, but I wanted to know who was behind the attack. Please go upstairs and tell Ava I am well attended to and have someone keep an eye on my car. I will pay them well."

Adil was feeling light-headed with the loss of blood and hailed a taxi to take him to Parsee General Hospital. It was the only place he could think of at the time.

Lungri hobbled up the stairs, leaning heavily on her crutch and knocked on Jer's door. The door flew open with an anxious and crying Ava eager to know how Adil was. Lungri apologized to Ava for her son's actions. Ava reassured her that she had done no wrong and did not need to apologize. Lungri conveyed Adil's message.

"But where did he go, Lungri?" Ava asked.

"Sorry *Memsahib*, he did not say, I only saw him taking a taxi. He wanted you not to worry and told me to tell you he was "well- attended to.""

"Please *Memsahib*," pleaded Lungri, "Try not to be sad, I have seen you together… so you worry, but he is a strong man and I am sure he will be fine."

Adil went to Parsee General Hospital, where he was seen to. He had a deep gash on his hand, stab wounds in the rib area and a fractured collar bone. His arm in a sling and his stab wounds treated, he carefully edged himself into a taxi and went home, planning on getting his car picked up the next day.

Paying the taxi driver, he unsteadily wound his way up the stairs to his flat, still dazed and light-headed from the events of the night. He fished out his flat keys from his blood-stained pocket, and headed for the bathroom where he washed off as much blood as he could manage with his unslung hand. Then carefully slipped into a clean pair of pajamas and finally into the deep comfort of his bed. The throbbing in his shoulder reminded him the next morning of the events of the night before.

"Good morning darling," a cheery Ruby said pulling back the drapes. Ruby turned to confront Adil at his lack of response. Seeing him lying silently in bed with his arm in a sling and blood on the sheet, she recoiled in mock horror.

"Oh God! what happened to you?" feigning shock and concern at his injuries.

He did not let on that he knew she had ordered the attack on him. Dealing with Ruby would come later, he thought with cold fury.

Chapter 27
The Plan for Ava

"Hello, am I speaking to Mr. Darius Byramji, Ava's father?" asked an agitated Ruby.

"Yes, this is he, and who am I speaking to?"

"This is Ruby, Adil Irani's fiancée?"

"What can I do for you, Miss uh, Ruby?"

"Keep your daughter away from Adil, she is interfering with our wedding plans!"

"My daughter would never do that!"

"Look, I am sure she is your pride and joy, carefully cultured and raised with all the correctness of a teacher, but she is getting in the way of my fiancée and I!" she said spitting out her words.

"Did you say he is your fiancée?"

"Yes! Yes! that is exactly what I said," she yelled.

Darius felt like he had been sucker-punched.

"We do not find Adil suitable for marriage to my daughter, so there is nothing to discuss Ms. Ruby... please keep our family out of your business and do not contact me again," he said with finality.

"I will hound you at all times of the day and night, Mr. Darius, until your daughter stops seeing my fiancée. Be very sure of that!"

Ruby hung up and then in an angry frenzy, she smashed the phone till it was in smithereens.

Darius realizing that Ava's mother's strict instructions of forbidding Ava from seeing Adil again, had not been heeded, felt the matter urgent enough for him to find a permanent solution to this impending scandal and disgrace to his family.

His plans for Ava to marry a prominent doctor that he and his wife felt was a suitable match were now in disarray. A whiff of scandal that indicated Ava was involved with someone else's fiancée would jeopardize their introduction and possible marriage.

As threatened, Ruby had kept up her barrage of daily phone calls to Ava's father, calling him at the most inconvenient of hours until the desired effect of unnerving him and his wife, was achieved. Ava was banned from seeing Adil.

Ruby breezed into Eruch's office, sitting on the edge of his desk and nonchalantly dangling her legs, back and forth. It was barely 10 am. but the morning sun was already unbearably hot when Darius knocked on the door of Eruch's office.

"Come in," Eruch said in a loud voice.

Darius entered, squinting at the seeming darkness of Eruch's office after the dazzling sunshine outside. He carried a large bag of goodies for Eruch.

"Darius, please have a seat," Eruch said pointing to the hard, wooden, government-issued chair. With a gesture of his hand, he turned and said "This is my friend Ruby."

Even before Eruch introduced Ruby to him, Darius had guessed that the woman in the skin-tight, short, black skirt, and low-cut blouse with a frill around the neckline, who had just jumped off the side off Eruch's table, was Ruby.

Darius offered her a limp handshake and hiding his instinctive dislike, said, "Ruby, how fortunate you are here. I wanted to assure you, and of course, my dear friend Eruch that no contact will take place between my daughter and Adil. I have seen to it."

Ruby and Eruch glanced at each other, Ruby trying not to behave like a cat that had just swallowed a canary.

"Do you mean your daughter does not know Adil is recuperating from his injuries?" inquired Ruby, looking away, pretending to pay close attention to her nails.

Darius's furrowed brow indicated his growing irritation with Ruby's feigned ignorance but he kept his composure and said,

"Ava only knows that Adil was attacked by some thug. She does not know what has happened to him since then."

Darius then cleared his throat and said, "Eruch, if you sign off on the money drafts on Ava's passport, I will have her on a plane to Canada, in the next few days."

He sighed then continued, "I may need your assistance in obtaining a fake marriage certificate too..."

Eruch said that he could arrange for that the same day and instructed Darius on where to pick up the document. He also gave him Ava's signed off passport.

Ava's dad wasted no time in collecting the fake marriage certificate and with the passport in hand, he directed the taxi driver to a Thomas Cook Travel office. Asking the taxi to wait, he went in and purchased a one-way ticket for Ava, from Bombay to Montreal, Canada, via London, England.

The stage was set for Ava to be made to believe the unthinkable, that Adil had caved in and married Ruby.

Jumping back into the waiting taxi, he headed for Jer's flat at Gowalia Tank, scowling at the thought of having to meet her.

Jer was surprised when the doorbell rang that morning and looking through the door slats, saw him standing there, tense and angry.

Opening the door, she called out to Ava to alert her that her dad was visiting. Ava came from her bedroom hoping her dad had finally agreed to her and Adil getting married and perhaps he had some news of Adil too.

Instead, declining a cup of tea that Jer offered him, he asked Ava to sit down.

"Why do you want me to sit down? Has something awful happened to Adil? Please tell me dad, please tell me it's not so," she said in a frantic voice.

"Now calm down, Ava," he said with urgency in his voice. "I have met with Eruch and he has given me your passport with his signature."

"Oh Daddy! That is wonderful news," she said jumping up and down, clapping her hands with joy.

He continued quietly, "Ava, I have some bad news for you... Adil and Ruby are married and have gone on their honeymoon. I thought it best that you leave as soon as possible for London to visit with your brother Aspi and then on to Montreal, where you have friends."

"I do not believe it, she said, reeling with shock. "Adil would not do that to me!"

Ava's father said, "Ava, he just used you to make Ruby jealous and ensure that she marries him. She's been putting him off for years, so I guess this was his solution. Look, I have a copy of their marriage certificate."

Ava looked at the document through tear-filled eyes, her mouth weighted with disbelief and sorrow. She had never seen a marriage certificate before and could barely read it through her blur of tears. After seeing the certificate, she gripped her dad's shirt, inconsolable, convulsed with sobs. Darius choked up, seeing the pain this news had caused his daughter, and was close to tears himself.

She would get over it in time, he thought. He was doing this for her own good.

Ruby made sure Adil did not leave the apartment or send any type of message to Ava. Adil was frustrated and angry at Ruby fighting every effort he made to leave the flat.

"Ruby, I will never ever marry you! Try all your tricks but know with certainty that you and I are never marrying in this lifetime! I know you actually stooped low enough to get a thug to try and scare me from seeing Ava!"

He fumed and went on "Well, here is some news for you... I will not only find a way of seeing Ava again, I promise I will make her my wife. How is that for a solemn promise?"

Adil hobbled to the door, managed to unbolt it with one hand and finally got out of the flat into the hallway and down the first stair.

"Get back in the flat at once!" screamed Ruby following him.

"I am taking a taxi to see Ava and will never see you again. Keep the damn flat and go to hell!" replied an angry Adil.

The neighbors had leaned out of their flats to see what the commotion was about but decided to keep away from the bickering couple.

"Adil! I am going to get you hurt worse than you are now, if you do not get into the flat right now!" she shouted.

"Go call your thugs on me, I am not afraid of them or anything you do to me!" he shouted back.

Ruby went to the stairs, gripping Adil's good arm and shoving him. He jerked away from her and losing his balance went tumbling down the stairs, his head hitting each stair with sickening thuds. Her hands covered her mouth, her face drained of all color.

When she pushed him, Adil had lost his footing on the stairs and with the hindrance of the sling on his hand could not manage to break his fall. He lay motionless on the landing at the bottom of the stairs.

Blood poured from a large gash on his head, one leg bent at an ugly angle.

Ruby ran to phone for an ambulance. It arrived after twenty long minutes... The paramedics quickly assessed his injuries and raced him to Parsee General Hospital.

Chapter 28
Adil in Hospital

Ruby did not accompany Adil in the ambulance. She was afraid she may be charged by police for being responsible for his injuries. That did not happen. When she told them it was an accident, the ambulance staff simply focused on Adil.

She phoned Eruch, giving him her version of what had happened to Adil, and asked him to accompany her to the hospital. Eruch had listened, making sympathetic noises, while she described the events that had taken place.

Ruby shivered longing for the reassurance of Adil but she realized with horror, he was likely dead and there was no one to blame but herself. For the first time in her life Ruby was frightened. What if the police found out she had ordered the hit on Adil or that the scuffle on the stairs caused his serious injuries?

Jumpy and with frayed nerves, she tried to focus on what she should do to try and right matters.

She called Adil's brother Rusi to tell him only that Adil was at the Parsee General Hospital. Rusi had many questions but Ruby insisted she had no knowledge of how his injuries had come about.

Arriving at the hospital several hours later, hanging on to Eruch's arm, she tiptoed along the long corridors finally arriving at Adil's ward. Cautiously slipping into the room, she saw Adil lying in bed as if he was in a deep sleep, with an array of tubes protruding from his body and monitors flashing.

"He is breathing," she said in a relieved whisper, squeezing Eruch's arm so hard that he winced.

Rusi acknowledged her presence, silently nodding in her direction. He avoided her eyes, struggling hard to contain his anguish at Adil lying comatose in front of him.

"Were you able to speak to Adil?" she whispered, hoping Rusi had not talked to Adil before he had been medicated. Only Adil knew of her part in giving him the fatal shove and her ordering the hit on him.

Before Rusi could answer, the doctor in charge of Adil's care, walked into the ward.

"Are you all family?" he asked.

"Yes, doctor," they both replied in unison.

The doctor paused, choosing his words carefully, "We've done several tests since Mr. Irani arrived, including a CAT scan of his head where he has sustained the most serious injury. His brain has swollen and since you gave permission," he said pointing to Rusi, "we have operated on him and removed a part of his skull. This will ease the pressure on his brain."

The doctor went on, "He is in a coma and he will stay that way until he decides to come out of it. We have the best specialists here at the Parsee General and are working as a team in monitoring and treating him."

Ruby asked, "So doctor, do you have any idea how long he will stay this way? When he comes out of the coma, will he be able to function normally?"

The doctor paused turned his head to face Ruby and thoughtfully asked, "How may I ask, are you related to Mr. Irani?" "I am his fiancée." Ruby replied, emphasizing the word "Fiancée."

"Well, his prognosis could change from day to day, he may be in a coma for days, weeks, months or longer. With injuries to the brain, we cannot say with certainty, at what pace a patient will recover."

The doctor paused again, and then said, "Since you are his fiancée, you should also be prepared for a fairly long recuperation period, if and when, he comes out of his coma."

Rusi thanked the doctor, then asked, "Is there anything at all I can do to speed his recovery?"

"Nothing at present, we will monitor him," replied the doctor, and left.

In the ensuing silence, each person digested what they had just heard in their own way. Rusi took leave from his job and was at Adil's side almost the entire day and night. He looked so broken, with his bandaged head and fractured shoulder, thought Rusi, twisted with sorrow.

Weeks passed with Adil showing no signs of lucidity. Refusing to give up hope, Rusi continued quietly speaking to him about important events in their past, playing music he knew Adil had enjoyed and holding his hand.

He saw to it that all the therapists and doctors that could help Adil were actively doing their part, truly believing Adil would return to normal when his brain had healed, however long it took. This was his younger brother who had come through many of life's trials intact. Deep sorrow streamed through him. He knew with profound conviction that he would always be at Adil's side with loving support.

Chapter 29
Ruby's Getaway

The cigarette glowed in the darkness of the living room as Ruby sat crouched in a corner of the bedroom, with her knees pulled up to her chin. It had taken four matches to try and light the cigarette in her shaking hands. Her well-laid plans seemed as fragmented as the pieces of glass that had been on the living room floor. Without Adil, the flat that she had fought so hard to live in, felt hollow, every slight movement echoing the emptiness of life without him.

The shifting shadows from the world outside unnerved her. Shuddering at the thought that karma was visiting her to settle scores, she pondered her next move and jumped when the cuckoo clock she had brought back from Switzerland, sounded at midnight. Her designated work horse was lying comatose in the hospital with no end in sight for his return.

For the first time she experienced feeling profoundly alone. Even the thought of Eruch or her other so-called friends yielded no comfort. After all they were as shallow as she was, lured by anyone susceptible to their sexuality. Suddenly her life felt shabby and soiled, realizing none of them really cared about her welfare.

Adil was of no use to her now. He belonged with the broken glass, swept away and discarded. Keeping up the pretense of caring deeply for Adil and their future together was an essential component of her new plan. This new plan was to save face with her family and his, on the off chance that the Australia plan did not work out.

It was time for a new beginning and with that in mind she checked the time difference between Sydney and Bombay. Ensuring that her long red polished nails were not damaged, she dialed Charles' number with a pencil. Eruch had managed to get her a phone connection. She did have some friends in right places, she thought with satisfaction.

Her left earring removed and on the bedside table, she listened to the Australian ring tone and smiled at the thought of Charles, one of the many lovers she engaged with, during her travels.

On the fourth ring Charles' deep baritone voice answered. "Hello?"

Using her most captivating voice Ruby said, "Darling Charles, its Ruby!"

"Hi gorgeous, which part of the world are you calling from?" asked Charles.

"You are the gorgeous one, Charles!" she replied with a laugh. "Charles darling, I have wonderful news!"

"What are you up to, you little vixen!" he teased in his heavily accented Aussie voice.

"I am coming to Sydney tomorrow!" Ruby exclaimed.

"Wonderful honey, you have kept me waiting long enough!

Get here as quickly as you can! Looking forward to it," he said smiling to himself.

"Charles darling, I am going to give you a thousand kisses, among other surprises..." Ruby purred into the phone. "I can hardly wait to be in your arms again." She hoped to make him even more fervent in welcoming her.

"Charles, honey, you know this is a huge move for me, so would you be an angel in finding me a suitable apartment and anything else I may need?" Ruby asked in her little girl, pretty-please, voice.

"I will see to absolutely everything, you just have to get on the plane and into the huge hug that awaits you," he said. There was that charming Aussie accent again, she thought with a smile.

He had many questions for her, but she suggested they have an intimate talk, snuggled up next to each other, after she arrived.

She heaved a huge sigh of relief! Putting down the phone, she hugged herself with self-satisfaction. Well, that assured a soft landing in Sydney, she thought smugly.

Now that Charles was in her corner, Ruby planned to slip away from Bombay as gracefully as she could. She wanted to create the illusion that she was still very much in love with Adil, and just going away for a short while, to ensure their opportunities in Sydney were not lost while he recuperated.

Next, she booked a one-way ticket to Sydney. Yes, she had her visa for permanent residency, she told the booking clerk on the phone. She had a free ticket because she had worked as a flight attendant with Air India.

"Bravo Ruby," she thought, pleased with herself.

Dressing quickly, she took a taxi first to her parents, then to the hospital where she was sure Adil's brother would be present.

She was going to keep her story simple but compelling. She was needed in Sydney to ensure that everything she and Adil had planned and put in place, remained intact and also to ensure that their permanent residency permit did not expire. With a somber expression on her face, she indicated that she would explain Adil's accident and have the Australian Immigration extend his visa.

Rusi listened, nodding his head, digesting her story. *He did not believe a word she said.*

Adil's brother, Rusi could see through her shallow, selfish intentions and the fact that she was dumping Adil at this crucial time, because he had ceased to be of use to her.

Though she said she would return in a few weeks, Rusi guessed that Ruby would not be back, unless she had some ulterior motive in doing so. He silently hoped that she would never return to blight his brother's happiness. Good riddance to bad rubbish, he thought. Finally, Adil was going to be free of her and through Ruby's own volition! He mentally cheered for his brother.

After a few minutes of fidgety hesitation, Ruby asked Rusi, "Do you have any news of Ava?"

"None," he replied indicating silently his reluctance to discuss the matter any further.

Ruby pretended to look sad as she slowly backed out of Adil's hospital ward. Once out in the corridor, she walked quickly to a waiting taxi to visit Eruch. He would have more up-to-date information, she figured.

"Hi Erruuuch, she said drawing out his name in a provocative manner, as she entered his office.

"Hello darrrrling!" said Eruch, jumping out of his chair to hug her as tightly as he could.

"You are going to love me, Ruby!" he said, biting his knuckles with suppressed glee.

"Eruch, I already love you, come on spill it!"

"Ava is on a plane to Canada, as we speak!" he said, hardly able to contain himself. "And... and, wait it gets even better. Ava's parents are on their way back to South Africa!"

"Eruch, I love you, this is the best news, ever!" Ruby exclaimed, delighted that her plan had been so successful.

"Wait Ruby, the news gets even richer!" said Eruch.

"Can it really get any better?" asked Ruby, jumping up and down.

"Yes, yes, listen to this... Ava left thinking Adil had jilted her and married you!" he said.

"The final nail in Ava's coffin!" exclaimed Ruby, doing a happy dance. "Eruch darrling," drawled Ruby, blowing him kisses, "you handled this like a pro!"

Eruch looked up blushing, shaking his head, himself surprised at the turn of events, lapping up the praise and attention she was lavishing on him.

Taking a last look around the flat she once dreamt of living in and was now impatient to leave, she called her parents to say goodbye. She had gone to such lengths to thwart Ava marrying Adil and she need not have. Fate had stepped in and done the work for her or so she thought!

She now had Charles in her sights and the careful molding of him as her work horse would begin soon after she landed in Sydney.

The numerous large bags of luggage would not fit in the boot of the taxi, so she asked the taxi driver to pile them into the back seat. She would ride up in front with him.

"*Memsahib* will ride in the front seat?" the taxi driver asked incredulously. It was unusual for a woman riding alone to sit next to a male taxi-driver.

Ruby snapped, "Take me to the airport and make it fast, unless you want me to take another taxi."

The taxi driver waggled his head, "No, no, *Memsahib*, I am happy to take you to the airport. Be assured I will get you there very fast."

The plane was on time and because of her Air India contacts, she was allowed all the luggage she wanted to take.

As the plane took off into the dark night, Ruby looked ahead, and laughed. Her new life had begun, and without a sickly Adil as an albatross around her neck. Yes, she had played her cards right, she figured, smugly satisfied with herself. Arranging the pillow and blanket to her comfort, she settled in for the long flight to a new chapter in her life.

She would have to think of a way to make Charles more amenable to her demands. But that would wait. All the thinking had made her weary and yawning loudly, she napped until dinner was served.

Chapter 30
Finding Solutions

For days Ava waited for Adil, in agony, not knowing why he did not call. Her heart ached more profoundly than she knew it ever could. Her early years of illness had been painful, but this torment was unbearable, she thought. She felt desperate for some news of him but each morning brought another void of information. When she was all cried out, stumbling through each day in a fog of misery, with no way to contact him, her imagination began to run wild, conjuring up awful possibilities.

Had she done something to make Adil angry with her?
Had he just found her parents rejection of him too much?
Did he feel unsure of choosing her over Ruby?
What could keep him away like this?

Jer's doorbell rang in the late afternoon. She peered through the slats wondering who it could be at that odd hour. All the day vendors had come and gone in the morning.

"What do you want?" she demanded, shaking her head in disapproval at the pavement dweller who stood outside her door. The cheek of her showing up on our doorstep, thought Jer, clenching her jaw.

"May I please speak to Ava *Memsahib*?" Lungri asked.

"How do you know the *Memsahib*?" Jer asked irritated that a pavement dweller would know Ava by name!

"Please go away," she said agitated.

But Lungri stood there balancing on her one crutch, showing no sign of moving.

Frustrated, Jer called out "Ava! Come here right away!"

Ava was sitting crestfallen in the bedroom. She came down the hallway, but seeing the look of irritation on Aunt Jer's face, turned around, hesitant to receive any negative news.

"I think you have a visitor," Jer said to Ava, pointing to the still unopen door, while nervously picking at her elbow, which Ava knew was a sure sign her aunt was annoyed.

Ava opened the door, surprised to see Lungri, who greeted her with a Namaste.

"What is it Lungri?" she asked hopefully.

"Do you have some news for me?"

Lungri looked down and sadly shook her head, "No *Memsahib* I have no news. I apologize for my son's actions... it was not the way I brought him up," she said, wiping away her tears with her sari.

Day after day came and went in a vacuum. The silence regarding Adil's whereabouts grew more ominous.

In the past, baking had always eased Ava's stress. She began to bake, going from cupcakes, to German Tortes, to cookies. Although Aunt Jer and Uncle Homi loved all her delicacies, Ava felt as tense as before. The aroma of freshly baked bread and macaroons filled the flat, but did nothing to make her feel any better.

Summoning her disciplined inner steel that had got her through tough times in the past, she resolved to do something meaningful with her time and energy. Her own situation had intensified her desire to try and alleviate the hopelessness of the pavement dwellers that society seemed to have turned their backs on. After some soul searching, she felt sure her decision to try and help the Untouchables was the right one. She discussed her aspirations with Aunt Jer, who as expected, was horrified at her plan. However, seeing the pain in her niece's eyes she said, "Well child, if it will make you happy... and take your mind of Adil..."

Ava immediately brightened and asked, "Would you employ Sita? She has no husband, and is torn between seeing to Mithu, who is now at the crawling stage, and going to work."

Jer tightened her lips. "How did she manage before?" she demanded.

Ava said, "I spoke to her a while ago," she paused and looked away, hearing Jer tut-tutting her disapproval.

"She said that while Mithu was a baby, she would bathe and feed him, put him to sleep and then leave him wrapped in a blanket on the pavement. Between jobs, she would hurry back in time for his next feeding. Now that he was crawling, she was at her wits end, as to what to do with him, while she worked."

Aunt Jer paced up and down the hallway, picking at her elbow as she considered Ava's request.

She did use a lady to clean her spacious flat and was not enthralled with her cleanliness, she thought... then again to have a stranger with a baby in her home... she would never have considered that!

Feeling anxious, Ava said, "Aunt Jer, all I am asking is that you give it a try and see if its works for you."

"I can't believe I'm even considering this!" Jer said throwing up her arms.

When Ava wrung her hands with a pleading look, she reluctantly agreed.

"Just a try..." she said, warning her niece not to raise her hopes of it working out.

A chance is all Ava needed. She flew down the stairs, crossed the road and went straight to Sita. Mithu had woken up from his nap and lifted his plump arms, his dimpled face gurgling and smiling. Ava picked him up, cradling him, while speaking to his mother about the trial arrangement.

Sita gasped and said, "*Memsahib*, I cannot believe it! Work right across the street from here? Bring Mithu to work? *Memsahib*, how can I thank you, this is like a dream come true for me. I was about to send Mithu away to the village, but my heart did not want to part with him. I promise you, I will work very hard and keep Mithu quiet, so he will not disturb the big *Memsahib*."

The next morning, Ava opened the door to Sita and Mithu, who looked clean like a bright new penny with his little tuft of hair neatly parted and combed. Aunt Jer gave Sita a doubtful look.

Sita left her worn sandals outside the door and gingerly entered the flat, wide-eyed at its spaciousness. Her heels were deeply cracked and the silver ankle bracelets clinked as she stepped into the hallway.

Mithu reached out a friendly arm to Aunt Jer, but she ignored him.

Ava accompanied Aunt Jer who was valiantly trying to dispel the discomfort she felt, as she took Sita around the huge flat, indicating the tasks she wanted her to complete. Sita listened intently and assured the big *Memsahib* that she would do exactly as she asked, pulled her saree further over her head and thanked her with a silent Namaste.

Over the next couple of days, Ava noticed Aunt Jer watching little Mithu with an entranced look on her face. She sensed Aunt Jer longed to hold Mithu and play with him but was reticent to show it.

Aunt Jer had no children of her own and though extremely hesitant at first, she realized that a baby is a baby, whether it be the progeny of a pavement dweller or her own. Mithu was a dimpled cutie with a sunny disposition, and Ava was pleased she was able to make one pavement dweller's life easier.

Ava turned her attention to the next pavement dweller... the one-legged Lungri.

When Ava asked Lungri how she could help her, the answer surprised Ava.

"I need many things *Memsahib*, you cannot give me what I want," Lungri said with a bitter laugh.

"Let me try, Lungri," replied Ava with conviction.

"*Memsahib*, I wished that my son Raju would be educated, but he has disgraced me by becoming a thug. Now I have no support in my old age. I am so tired these days. I wish to return to my village near Lucknow, and live there quietly."

Ava asked, "How much money would you need?"

Lungri thought about it and shook her head, "It's too much, *Memsahib*, unless I can find work there."

"How close to Lucknow is your village?" Ava asked.

"It's actually one train stop away from Lucknow, *Memsahib*," Lungri replied, dubious that Ava, however well-intentioned, could lift a pavement dweller off the streets of Bombay!

"Lungri, I have an aunt in Lucknow who has eleven children. If she needs help, would you go to Lucknow?"

"I cannot afford the fare," Lungri said sadly, not expecting any of Ava's ideas to actually take shape.

Ava said, "Lungri, take a day or two to think about it and if you really feel life would be better for you in Lucknow, I will arrange work for you, pay your train fare and give you some money."

Lungri was startled into silence. She could not fathom why anyone would want to do this for an Untouchable like her. Lungri dismissed Ava's offer as being a pipe dream. A convenient story ending like in the movies, she thought bitterly, but not real. Spitting out the paan (betel leaf) she had been chewing, she put it out of her mind.

After a few days, Ava approached Lungri again.

"Lungri, have you considered the possibility of going back to Lucknow?"

Lungri looked at Ava in disbelief. Was Ava crazy, she wondered? After all she had been shunned by almost everyone except fellow Untouchables. This time Lungri though hardened by life, realized that crazy or not, Ava was serious and that life may be throwing her a rare opportunity to get off the pavement.

Her response startled Ava, "*Memsahib*, what can I do for you and your man?"

A look of anguish passed over Ava's face, when Lungri said 'your man.'

"Please pray for us," she replied in a shaky voice choking with tears. Regaining her composure, she asked "Lungri, why are you hesitant... what are you afraid of?"

"I do not want to leave Raju behind and I do not know where to find him!" she said hardly believing her words.

"We could leave a note for him with your neighbor Sita," Ava suggested.

Still Lungri was reluctant, even though the last time she had seen her son was on the day Adil was assaulted. What if he needed her? she reasoned.

"Lungri, could you leave him a note that he will find when he comes to drop off some money for you?" asked Ava, wondering if Lungri was just too toughened by life on the pavement to handle a radical lifestyle change.

Lungri nodded sadly. She really would have wanted to hug her son and tell him in person of her plan to live in Lucknow. She cried, wiping her tears with her faded cotton saree.

Ava was amazed at the bond between mother and son. Despite the fact that Lungri knew her precious son was a thug, she still loved him.

Lungri wrapped her well-worn sarees into a bundle, left a note to Raju in the box that held her precious few possessions against the iron fence of the park and giving a last look around, walked away.

Ava gave her money for a bus to the train station, a ticket to Lucknow she had purchased, and a little money to tide her over until she started working. She also gave her a letter of introduction to her aunt. Knowing her aunt always grumbled that she was unable to find reliable help, Lungri would be a godsend.

Ava and Lungri said goodbye with a solemn Namaste.

When Ava got home a pleasant surprise awaited her. Aunt Jer was taking her long after lunch nap on the couch, in the living room. Contentedly asleep with his chubby arms hugging her was Mithu. Ava looked at the unlikely sight and felt a sense of fulfilment. Jer had grown so fond of both Sita and Mithu, that she had taken the bold step of asking them to move into her spare bedroom. Sita still felt comfortable sleeping on the floor but now they were sheltered from the elements.

Each had enriched the life of the other. Pavement dweller and rich aunt together, sharing comfort and joy.

Rani's daughter Devi, was now the only one left on the pavement in front of Ava's window. Her lazy father had disappeared and her brothers and Raju had joined forces in pickpocketing and thuggery. The daughter had received some money for a dowry from her mother, Rani. She would stealthily, under cover of darkness, give her daughter as much money as she could get from her rich lover. Devi was just a teenager and her being all alone on the pavement was extremely dangerous.

Ava had discussed the girl's plight with Lungri who had told her that she felt the best course of action for Devi was to send her to relatives in the village of Kanpur. Kanpur had a cottage industry where the women of the village wove textiles and made them into clothing items which in turn were sold to tourists in the market. It also had a vocational school for the village people, where she could learn a skill and possibly find gainful employment.

Meeting Ava one night, her face totally covered with her saree, Rani had given Ava her blessing to send her daughter to Kanpur. Though her sons and husband had long since disappeared, Rani's shame at leaving her family for her wealthy lover, had never diminished. She would always be their mother and felt she had let them down.

Pushing through the dense crowd of people at the train station, Ava made contact with Devi. Buying her a train ticket to Kanpur and ensuring the dowry money her mother had given her and some money for her relatives Ava had given her, was safely tucked into her bodice. She hugged the young Devi and with a final Namaste, waved at her as her train chugged out of the station.

Having seen to Lungri, Rani's daughter Devi, Sita and Mithu, Ava's attention returned to her helplessness at not knowing Adil's whereabouts.

Weeks had gone by with no news of Adil. The last she had seen or heard from him, he had been assaulted and bleeding from injuries. She wished she could be at his side, lovingly taking care of him in every way she could.

Chapter 31
Ava's Parents' Decision

When she did not hear from Adil for two weeks, Ava began to believe that he had indeed married Ruby.

She begged her father to allow her to go back to Durban. She needed the healing company of her friends there, especially Kay. So much had happened since she and Kay had shopped for a trousseau, amid laughter, cups of tea and delicious homemade confections. Neither of them had imagined it would turn out to be a painful mess. She thought fondly of the fun times she had shared with Kay, always quick to find humor in any situation.

But Ava's parents refused to let her return to Durban.

"There are no young Parsee men of marriageable age in Durban," Ava's father said.

"Eventually you will get yourself attached to someone who is not a Parsee and cause another set of problems. No, my dear daughter, you must be brave, as you have shown yourself to be in the past, and make your future in Canada."

Ava looked on with a blank expression.

He went on, "I have informed your cousin in Toronto of your arrival. He has a lovely home and is well connected in the community. I have asked him to ensure you meet eligible Parsee gentlemen, and he is happy to oblige."

Suddenly Darius's forehead creased in a worried expression, realizing a huge oversight in his plans.

"There may be a problem of him meeting you at the airport... he is in Toronto and you are going to Montreal!"

"What? How will she manage alone, Darius?" asked a perturbed Dina.

Darius was silent. He hadn't figured that out and had no answer.

"My friend Jackie is in Montreal. We were friends at school in Durban. She will surely pick me up at the airport," said Ava dryly. "Our cousin cannot be expected to come from Toronto to Montreal just to meet me at the airport. For now, it will be Jackie that I shall be depending on. I will phone her when I get to London."

Ava knew her fate was sealed and had to accept her parents' deciding her immediate future. She could rebel all she wanted but her father held the purse strings. Disobeying him would mean she would be stranded in India, with no money or passport.

He held both.

"Ava, there is a week to go before your flight to Canada. Ruby has proven to be a loose cannon and is not to be trusted. She has harassed us night and day and we fear for your safety. Its best she not know where you are residing."

Ava did not want to leave Aunt Jer and the comfort of her company. Darius paused, noticing Ava's lip turn down in disappointment, but carried on talking to Ava in a soothing tone.

"In the interim, I have arranged to have you stay at a luxurious flat belonging to a Parsee widow. It has a large airy bedroom and a balcony that overlooks the ocean. You will move there today and stay until it's time to drive to the airport."

Giving up any expectation of hearing from Adil, melancholy set into her soul. She wished she were dead. She would gladly walk on hot coals, if she could find Adil but had no inkling where he might be. When she asked her parents or Aunt Jer, they were silent. Eventually, she stopped asking them about Adil.

The marble tiles felt cool and calming under her bare feet as she walked from the bedroom to the balcony. Ava could hear the waves crash against the rocks directly under her balcony.

By their rhythmic lapping against the rocks, she knew the ebb and flow of the tides.

They were calling to her, come, come to us, we will embrace you and all your pain will be gone. Swish, swish, swish, jump into our cool embrace, swish, jump into our cool water and find peace.

She looked down at the jagged rocks and wondered if she could be sure, they would take her life away, or would they too let her down, lingering in pain. Desolate, she decided she could not trust them either. Her heart stored up the weight of unshed tears as she waited for her departure from India, and Adil.

Chapter 32
Ava Leaves for London

On a beautiful balmy day in December, Ava was driven to the airport. She requested a brief stop at Jer's flat. Going from window to window, in the hallway, she remembered the life-changing events of the past eight months.

The beep, beep of Adil's car horn and his sunshine smile as he looked up at her, streaming love. She gazed at the empty pavement, without the pavement dwellers. She hoped they were living an uncomplicated, contented life, free from the mean streets of Bombay.

With all her silk and diamonds, she was anguished and lonely, she thought, with a twinge of bitterness. She would have happily exchanged all her privilege for a simple, happy life with Adil.

She had come to Bombay, loathing the idea of the stench, the crowds and the air and noise pollution. Now that she was leaving it, she realized just how much the simple pavement dwellers had taught her about what was really important in life. The wealthy people living in these huge sprawling apartments thought they were superior to the pavement dwellers.

The building *only* shielded them from the elements, like rain, but *not* from heartache. Pain hammered down on her heart and there was nothing to shield her from its onslaught.

Although she missed seeing the pavement dwellers every day, she felt a deep satisfaction knowing she had tried to assist them, towards a better place in life.

Feeling as if she'd been sentenced for a crime she had not committed, Ava sat with her mother and Aunt Jer at the airport, while her dad saw to her luggage, tickets and boarding pass. Not even Aunt Jer who always supported and soothed her, could do or say anything to assuage her pain. In the waiting lounge though it was stifling hot, she felt cold and shivery.

Her mother said, "Remember, my lovely, brave daughter, when God closes one window, He opens another."

When it was time to board, she woodenly hugged her dad, mum and Aunt Jer. Hearing the announcement of her flight, she picked up her hand luggage and went to the desk, where they checked her boarding pass and welcomed her onto the flight.

Ava's flight to London was sleepless with a restless unease. Her newly married brother Aspi and his wife were at the airport to greet her. Although she returned their greetings, she felt lifeless, like a zombie composed of crushed glass, going through the motions. Smiling when she felt she was supposed to, trying to act the part of a sister en route to Montreal.

Since it was a few days before Christmas, Aspi and his wife spoke of baking batches of shortbread cookies.

Later that evening, they had planned to attend a neighbor's party and Ava offered to make a trifle, something she made umpteen times before.

An hour later, her brother saw her standing at the stove, where she had gone to make custard for the trifle. She was staring blankly ahead of her, unable to remember how to make the basic custard.

"Are you okay, Ava?" Aspi asked, repeating his question with growing concern when it elicited no response from her.

Realizing that all was not well with his sister, he put his brotherly arm around his sister and guided her towards the bedroom. Filling a red rubber hot water bottle, he tucked her into bed with it.

"Oh Aspi! I'm sorry," Ava apologized, starting to sob.

"Ava, I do not know all the details," Aspi said, "but I know something awful must have happened. Take all the time you need. Try and rest, you have had a long flight and when you feel better, come downstairs for some brandy," he said to cheer her up.

Ava held her brother's hand to her cheek and kissed his palm.

"Thank you," she said, feeling the comforting warmth of the hot water bottle, while tears flowed and were absorbed soundlessly into her pillow.

A week later, at London Heathrow airport, Ava's brother held her in a long, warm hug.

Ava asked, "Will you come to Montreal?"

His brow furrowed with concern for his sister, who seemed so very fragile in her newly purchased winter coat.

"Remember you can call me collect, as often as you need to. I love you. You're not alone," he said lovingly.

"Who will meet you at the airport?"

"Jackie, my old friend from Durban. I phoned her from your home, remember me asking if I could make a long-distance phone call?"

"Oh, yeah, yeah, I thought you may be calling mum and dad."

"I did call them to report my safe arrival and then called Jackie. Aspi, Jackie is amazing! She has already found me a furnished apartment around the corner from where she lives. She said she's made up a bed for me and even put some essentials in my fridge," said Ava with a happy laugh.

Aspi felt reassured. That laughter had a familiar ring to it. His sister was going to be all right...

Chapter 33
Ava's Arrival in Montreal

Snow fell softly at midnight, as the plane skidded slightly, before making a smooth landing at Montreal-Trudeau airport.

She spotted Jackie as soon as she stepped out of Customs and Immigration. Waving wildly with a huge grin, curly red hair and freckles dusted over her face.

"How are you, kid? It's good to see you!" she said wrapping Ava in a warm hug.

"Give me a bag, before you topple over trying to carry it all by yourself. Guess you have all the latest fashion inside! We have a lot of catching up to do kid!" she said as she piled the suitcases into the boot of her car.

"We sure do," replied a jet-lagged Ava.

"How do you feel about resting up tonight and we hit the town tomorrow for Sunday brunch?" asked a spirited Jackie.

"Sounds perfect. Come over and wake me up, okay?" Ava said.

It was around noon when Ava heard the doorbell ring repeatedly. Slipping on her robe she stumbled to the front door.

"Who is it?" she asked stifling a yawn and freezing in her bare feet. Why was she so tired she wondered?

"Open up, it's me, kid!" said Jackie in her usual upbeat manner.

Ava unlatched the door, letting in a whoosh of icy air. She shivered pulling the robe tighter around herself.

"Hey kid, hurry up and get dressed or we will miss brunch!" Jackie said, patting Ava on the back.

"Okay, give me fifteen minutes, I will be all yours!" Ava said, feeling a little more awake.

True to her word, fifteen minutes later Ava was washed, dressed and raring to go. The two friends trudged up the snowy Cote Des Neiges hill, bundled up against the winter cold.

Ava had come from extreme heat in India to minus zero-degree weather in Canada, exchanging sandals for boots, but she seemed to make the transition like a penguin to the sea.

"So, how are you feeling kid?" asked Jackie, her freckles on full display in the midday sun.

"Still jet-lagged but happy to be with you here in Montreal!" Ava said with exuberance.

"Yeah, Montreal is a pretty magical place as you will soon discover. It's a fun city and I think it's what the doctor ordered for you. Am I right?" asked an observant Jackie.

"Right on," said Ava, giving her friend's arm an affectionate squeeze.

Soon they were seated at a table in Le Papillon's, next to a large window, overlooking the steep hill they had just climbed. A friendly waitress came and took their order for Eggs Benedict, café au lait and at Jackie's urging a Pain au Chocolat.

"Okay kid, tell me all about your crazy bachelor introductions, and why you landed up alone in Montreal instead of some exotic honeymoon destination."

"It's a long story Jackie..."

"I like long stories especially from you, so spill it!"

Ava told Jackie how South African Apartheid had prevented her from attending a local university and her parent's anxiety at her possibly marrying a non-Parsee if she continued to stay in Durban, and their sudden unwillingness to send her to Dublin to study medicine. She told her about the pavement dwellers and their stories and finally how she had met Adil and then lost him.

Jackie listened intently.

"What made them want to send you to Montreal?" asked Jackie.

"Well, that was actually a mistake, my dad intended to send me to Toronto where I have a cousin, but he mistakenly booked the ticket for Montreal... can you believe it!"

"No kid I can't, why do you think a careful person like your dad would make a glaring mistake like that?"

"All I can put it down to is Fate, by its very nature it never does what we expect it to do, does it?"

Jackie roared with laughter, as Ava shook her head, happy that fate had stepped in and brought her to Montreal.

Jackie's forehead creased into a puzzle again.

"Why did they not send you to Dublin to study medicine?"

"That is still a mystery to me Jackie, I really do not know. It was such a sudden change of heart and dad's behavior was so strange, that I can only suspect a major business deal had gone awry. Financially embarrassed is all I can guess. Though, he did give me a generous bank draft and some Canadian dollars."

"Your Dad was wealthy. I hope it's just a temporary setback..." said Jackie, alarmed.

"Yes, it's been a very tough time all around and losing Adil..." said Ava, lips quivering.

Jackie could tell that the subject of Adil was a deep wound that had not healed. Steering the conversation in a more optimistic direction she said, "Well, shall we drink to fun in Montreal!" as she lifted her cup of café au lait.

Ava lifted her cup and clinked it with the ever-cheery Jackie, trying to chase away the threatening blues.

Jackie caught the eye of the waitress and to Ava's surprise ordered two flutes of champagne.

After the divine brunch of Eggs Benedict, café au lait, Pain au Chocolat topped off with a flute of champagne, Ava viewed her world in a happier, lighter mood.

Walking out of the restaurant into the fresh wintry air, Jackie asked Ava, "So what would you like to do now, perhaps see a movie?"

"Jackie, all I really would like to do is sleep, I just feel worn out!"

"It's jet-lag, kid. A few days of rest and you will be a bouncy ball again. Okay let's walk off our brunch and tuck you into bed!"

With that the two friends walked arm in arm down the hill, stopping at the LCBO, where Ava purchased a few bottles of wine, and a bottle each of Brandy and Bailey's liqueur.

As soon as she got home, Ava had slipped into warm pajamas and fluffy slippers.. Jackie poured them snifters of brandy and the happy friends clinked glasses and sat chatting till evening.

Chapter 34
Ava's Adjustment

When Jackie left, Ava snuggled into bed with the red hot water bottle, her brother Aspi, had thoughtfully packed in her suitcase. An overwhelming fatigue came over her and for the next several days she did nothing more than sleep.

Jackie popped by suggesting outings, but Ava kept declining.

"Hey kid you have got to eat something beside a few pastries and candy."

"I don't want to eat anything," Ava replied morosely.

"What is the matter, kid. Spill it, is something bothering you?

I know everything is new and strange around you but I am here to show you the city. Come on, let's have some fun!"

But Ava would not budge. She either slept or stared out of the window, unaware of time, day or night.

She was aware on some level that she had to get out of this funk and find a job. But that was left for the tomorrows that followed.

What she was thinking was "I need Adil, I need to know he is well. I need his love." But that was her silent battle that no one could understand.

"Hey kid, it's been a month since you arrived, and I don't know how to help you!" said an alarmed Jackie.

"Oh, I will be fine, Jackie. I just need a little adjustment time that is all."

"You have been saying that for a month and nothing has changed. I am worried about you, kid."

After a month of this behavior, Jackie brought a doctor to attend to Ava. The young physician entering her bedroom jolted Ava out of her indifference.

"Doctor I am fine, just getting used to the Canadian winter," she said with weak smile.

"In our Canadian winters we usually eat a little more than in summer," replied the doctor, solemnly continuing to examine her.

He spoke to her gently, urging her to try to eat some protein and get out in the fresh air.

"This is a prescription for medication that I think will help you, and do make an appointment to see me in my office in a few days." He turned to leave but stopped and scribbled his home phone number on his business card and handed it to Ava.

"Just in case you feel like talking to me, feel free to call." He left as quietly as he had come.

Ava knew she was in trouble, feeling like an ant that climbs up a wall, only to fall right back down. She had to try the medication, if only because Jackie had taken the trouble to bring the doctor to her.

She needed to dig into her toolbox of coping strategies and pull out "*brave*" and "*strong*." She was alone and had to stand on her own and not bother others with her pining for Adil.

The next day, Jackie entered Ava's apartment in a great state of excitement, saying "News, such news! I ran all three blocks to your apartment to tell you!" she was gasping for breath and reaching for a glass of water.

"Goodness Jackie, you sound like you just won the jackpot!" Ava said, taking her coat.

"Well, your guess is not too far-fetched. St. Mary's Hospital had a vacancy for a clerk at one of their clinics. I went in to speak to personnel and mentioned you. Guess what! A helpful lady there is keen to meet you! You have an interview tomorrow!"

"Tomorrow! gee Jackie, I am not sure I am ready," she said doubtfully. "I still feel a bit wobbly."

"Kid! this is just what you need to get rid of your "wobbles," said Jackie patting her reassuringly on the back.

She sat up straight and summoning her strong self said with conviction, "Jackie you are right! Its time I pulled myself up by my bootstraps and faced the world!"

Ava looked at her friend affectionately, "Wow, I won the jackpot of friendship, when I met you!"

In minutes, Ava had the makings of a chocolate cake mixed, and in the oven. The fragrance of baking filled the warm kitchen.

"Yum! what are you baking, Ava?" said Jackie relieved to see a semblance of her happy friend.

"Guess?" said a laughing Ava.

Soon the kettle was whistling, and the two friends were animatedly chatting and teasing each other, over cups of tea and large slices of chocolate cake.

Chapter 35
New Experiences

Wine, Food and Fun' is what Ava thought life in Montreal was all about and she loved it.

When Jackie said, "Ava, I haven't heard you laugh so heartily in a long time," she felt perhaps a measure of healing had slowly but surely taken place.

Ava had worked at the hospital for just over a year when the phone rang, summoning her to the Human Resources office. Hurrying there, her mind raced.

Had she made a mistake with a booking or been impolite to a patient? Had someone complained?

Perhaps her French needed to have more of a Quebecois French accent?

Reaching the Human Resources office, she lightly knocked on the door.

Her manager, a lady with hair greying at the temples and sporting oversized black horn-rimmed spectacles that hung from a chain around her neck, pointed to a chair, saying, "Ava, first of all let me compliment you on your excellent work ethic." Then she paused, and with a steady look, said, "As you know, all hospital personnel are unionized."

Ava nodded her understanding.

"Well, the way it works is that when there is a budget cut back, which as you know there is, the last person hired, has to be the first one to be let go. I am truly sorry to say that person is you."

Ava was shocked. She had not seen this coming. She did not know what to do next, so she asked, "Where do I go now?"

The manager said, "We have collected your things, which you can pick up at the front desk, on your way home."

"Oh, thank you," Ava managed to say, walking out of the office in a daze. She collected her things at the front desk, where the receptionist gave her a look of pity.

Walking down the Cote Des Neiges hill to her apartment, she left her coat unbuttonedd. The sting of the cold air made her more aware of her surroundings, bringing focus to what had just taken place. Reaching her apartment, she threw off her coat and boots, filled a hot water bottle and curled up in bed.

Ava did not know how long she had been asleep, when she heard a persistent ringing. The doorbell rang again, joined by an insistent knocking on the door. As she stumbled to open it, she realized she was wearing yesterday's clothes.

"Who is it?" she asked, feeling out of sorts.

"It's Jackie kid, open the door, I am turning into an icicle out here."

Sheltering her eyes from the bright sunlight outside, she let Jackie in.

"Come here, kid," Jackie said, wrapping her in a hug. "I just found out about what happened at work yesterday. Why didn't you call me?" Jackie asked.

"I guess I fell asleep," Ava said, stifling a yawn and shuffling over to the sofa where she sat down heavily.

"It's all going to be okay, we'll find you another job in no time…you take it easy in the meantime, okay? Rest up and call me when you feel like getting out a bit, okay, kid?" Jackie said with a wide grin that made the freckles on her face seem like they were smiling too.

Ava did not call Jackie or anyone else. She had taken to her bed and slid into that slippery slope of depression. Her phone was off the hook, and the doorbell ignored, newspapers collected on her doorstep and mail jammed her overflowing mailbox, while she took refuge in her bed.

She said to herself, I need a rest. I will be fine after a few days. Need to take it easy. The days stretched into several weeks.

One morning she heard Jackie's voice saying, "Thank you, sorry for bothering you."

The woman that retreated looked like her landlady.

Jackie approached her bed, and said, "Ava, I have packed a few of your things and I am taking you to stay with my mum."

"What are you talking about, Jackie?" asked Ava, wiping the sleep from her eyes.

Jackie looked at her with a serious gaze.

"Ava, it's been three weeks since you took to your bed, your phone is off the hook, I had to ask the landlady to open the door for me. I can understand you are feeling awful, kid, but you cannot stay here alone. My mum wants you to come and stay with her for a while."

Ava's shoulders slumped, shaking her head. "I am fine, Jackie, just taking a rest that is all," she sighed, feeling this was entirely unnecessary.

Jackie replied, "Ava, you are definitely not fine. When did you last eat something?"

"Hmmm, don't remember, but I am fine. No need to bother your mum," Ava said, a little more alert now.

"Ava, please get up and let's get your coat and boots on. I am not taking any more 'I'm fine!' from you," said Jackie firmly. She took Ava's arm and helped her out of bed.

Ava almost toppled over; she could barely stand. Jackie helped Ava get on her boots and coat, picked up the bag of essentials she had packed and managed to get Ava into the car. Driving to her mother's apartment, she sounded very stern.
"Ava, you are staying with mum, till she says you are okay to be on your own."
"Okay, Jackie" replied Ava, in barely a whisper.

In the following weeks, time seemed to be of no importance. Jackie's mum called her to the kitchen for breakfast and when she just stared at it, she insisted she eat it. So, she did.

Ava was thinking of Adil and how much she missed him, needed him, wanted him. She remembered with a wistful smile that she was now free of her parents imposing their will on her, unshackled from their grip on her liberty. So why did she feel like a ship without direction, floating like some flotsam or jetsam?

Sitting in front of the window in Jackie's mother's small guest bedroom she realized she had to again open up her toolbox of coping strategies. Shaking off the clouds of blues she took out the three "tools" she needed, "*Survive,*" "*Innovate*" and "*Thrive.*"
Then she went to work on herself.

First, she went in search of Jackie's mother. She found her sitting in the welcoming kitchen, having a cup of tea.
Jackie's mother saw Ava hesitate at the doorway to the kitchen and got up to throw a warm arm around her shoulder and sat her down in the warm, welcoming kitchen, pouring them both steaming, fragrant cups of Earl Grey tea.

"Jackie told me about your ordeal in India," she said, sipping her tea, savoring its warm comfort, and eyeing Ava.

"I want you to remember this, God makes you and He matches you. Here love, have some gingerbread, it will warm you up!" she said as she pushed the plate of cookies towards Ava.

"Ava, Jackie and I love you. Have faith, smile, all will be well... in "His Time" not ours."

She smiled reassuringly and gently brushed Ava's cheek with her kind, worn hands.

Ava thought about her own mum and wondered if she would have supported her free lifestyle here, or would she and dad have imposed the same autocratic rules, as they did in Durban. She ached for their support, and knew from her mum's weekly letters that they loved her but were unable to accept the modern era.

She had to survive, innovate and thrive with her own steely resolve and God-given strengths.

Returning to her apartment she was determined to get back her health.

First, she enrolled at a gym and worked out daily, starting with fifteen minutes and working up to an hour.

Next, she started volunteering with Médecins Sans Frontières and felt her pulse quicken as she connected with personnel in the medical arena.

Even though her work was on the fringes of the medical field, she reveled in just being around doctors, nurses and the extended field personnel.

Her mind felt stronger, her thoughts clearer and her intentions more determined. She felt a surge of returning confidence.

The thought of looking for a job and working for someone else did not appeal to her. She needed to challenge herself and her abilities to feel alive again.

During her daily walk up the Cote des Neiges hill to St. Mary's Hospital, she had always admired a small flower shop and sometimes stopped to speak to the owner. The atmosphere in the shop reminded her of fragrant flowers, Adil and idyllic romance.

The owner greeted her warmly, "Bonjour! How are you? Where have you been?" he asked.

"You know my wife and I have decided to move to Toronto, because our daughter has married and settled there."

"What will you do with your store?" Ava asked.

"The landlord wants the store, so I simply have to sell my stock and I am ready to go," he replied in happy anticipation.

"I am happy for you, but I will miss your store," replied Ava, wistfully looking around the store as if she could memorize the landscape around her.

They chatted in French as always. She wondered how he would manage in English-speaking Toronto, but did not ask.

As she walked down the hill to her apartment, she saw a "For Rent" sign in a vacant store window. It was right across from the Jewish General Hospital and in close proximity to both St. Mary's Hospital and St. Justine Hospital. The intersection of Cote Des Neiges and Cote St. Catherine was a busy one. What a fabulous location for a business, she thought!

What type of business would do well here she wondered?

Her mind danced with possibilities, methodically examining each one with a growing sense of inspiration.

Deep in thought she reached home, feeling a *frisson* of excitement. Dare she? She had four thousand dollars saved up, barely enough start-up capital for any business. But the idea gathered momentum, racing forward, instead of going away.

A few hours later she phoned Jackie.

"Jackie, feel like coming over for a glass of wine and stay for dinner?"

"Sure kid, when do you want me over?" Jackie asked.

"How about now?" Ava replied with a laugh.

"Sure, I will be right over. May I bring something?" Jackie asked politely.

"Just your smile," said Ava, looking forward to a relaxing evening with her best friend.

By the time Jackie arrived, Ava had uncorked a bottle of Chianti and lit some candles. She took out the veal cutlets from the fridge, rolled them in herbed bread crumbs and had them sizzling in a pan with butter. The doorbell rang just as she drained the steamed asparagus and warmed up the aromatic basmati rice with a knob of butter.

She opened the door to a beaming Jackie, "Hi kid, you are cooking something delicious, mmm, let me guess."

"Let me take your coat, Jackie. Relax," Ava said as she handed Jackie a glass of Chianti.

Jackie sat in Ava's cozy kitchen, taking in the divine aromas of her cooking and smiling at the cheerful demeanor of her friend
. Ava had not mentioned Adil in the last few weeks and Jackie took that as a sign that she had healed from those terrible events.

Conversation flowed easily as Ava flipped over the veal, sprinkled it with some salt, freshly ground pepper and a generous squeeze of fresh lemon juice. Removing the veal, she threw into the same pan, sliced mushrooms and another knob of butter.

Jackie laid the table while Ava plated the warm veal, mushrooms, asparagus and rice, teasing, "Gee Ava, this is amazing and all in the few minutes it took me to get here! Are you sure this is an impromptu dinner?"

"Jackie, you know me well, I have been slaving over a hot stove, all day!" Ava replied with a wink.

"You know kid, you should be a chef," said Jackie nodding thoughtfully.

"Forget it! I only cook for select company" replied Ava, with a twinkle in her eye, lifting her glass in a toast to Jackie.

After dinner, Ava popped two of her frozen Chocolate Lava cakes into a hot oven and made them both frothy cappuccinos. While enjoying the melt in your mouth dessert and fresh coffee, Ava deliberated on how she would ask Jackie what her opinion was about a wild idea she had. The kernel of the idea seemed like a juggernaut racing ahead with a will of its own.

"Jackie, did you know there was a vacant store right across from the Jewish General Hospital?" she asked in a casual tone.

"I think so, is it the one that sold wheelchairs, walkers and other healthcare appliances?"

"Yes, that is exactly the one. It's vacant and has a 'For Rent' sign..." Ava trailed off...

"I want to rent it and open my own business!"

There, she had put words to her wild idea.

Jackie looked at her in stunned disbelief.

"Ava, we have both done some crazy things before... but this is scary crazy!"

"Jackie, I am serious and I know I have never run a business of my own... it is a risk... but what is life without a challenge?"

Jackie's response was to laugh till she began to hiccup. Her face flushed, she took a gulp of cappuccino and almost choked on it. Ava brought her a glass of water.

"Do you want me to drink the water or splash it on my face?" Jackie asked, going off on another uncontrollable fit of laughter.

"God, Ava, without you around, life sure would be a bore. With you, it's like driving a fast car on one of those hairpin bends in Europe, exhilarating and knuckle biting. But," she said, shaking her head, "you seem to thrive on challenges, so how are you going to pull this one off?"

"Jackie, I feel it's time to test myself. I've always felt I could successfully run my own business. If I never try, how will I know?"

"It's not applause I am looking for Jackie, its purpose, after all, what excitement is there in life if we don't show courage in the face of uncertainty?"

Jackie had recovered from her fits of laughter and gazed at Ava, shaking her head in amazement.

"I can see you're serious about this," she said at last.

Ava asked, "Would you like a snifter of brandy?"

"I think I *need* it!" replied Jackie chuckling.

They both sipped their brandy, quietly reflecting at this new development.

"Jackie, I figure if I am unshackled from my parents and their prejudices, I ought to use my life to some useful purpose. My dreams of becoming a doctor were suffocated. This is my chance to test my mettle and try to flourish in the face of all obstacles and uncertainties." She paused looking intently at her friend's reaction.

"Jackie, are you with me?"

Her face as flushed and pink as it could ever be, Jackie said, "Of course kid, I am with you, it's crazy but I am on board."

Jackie poured them glasses of Baileys and asked Ava to propose a toast.

"To courage!" she said as they clinked glasses.

Chapter 36
The Persian Garden

After her conversation with Jackie, Ava got her shop ready for business at lightning speed. Ava thrived with the challenges of each phase of this venture.

On a sunny, cold November morning The Persian Garden, Plant and Gift Boutique was born. The doorbell tinkled as the first customer came into the store, looking around at the wonderland that presented itself.

The windows were dressed for Christmas with a large Balsam Fir tree on the left-hand side of the window and mini boxwoods lined up along the length of the window. The trees were decorated with little silver bells, tiny glittering balls in silver, red and gold, red holly berries, reams of tinsel and the *piece de resistance*—mini gingerbread cookies iced in shapes of bells, stars, houses, and snowflakes, tied to the branches with colored ribbons.

The extravaganza of adorned trees glistening with dusted snow were met with oohs and aahs of delight by passersby. Shoppers quickly purchased the trees saying with glee how fortunate they felt to have found them.

Streaming down the walls were swathes of red velvet ribbon with pine branches, pine cones, holly and tiny frosted white lights. Elegant wreaths in a huge variety of pine, cedar and blue spruce hung on every spare inch of the store.

The glass shelves and tables had rows upon rows of shiny wrapped large and small poinsettias in a profusion of bright reds, pretty pinks and elegant whites.

Beside the counter were spools of ribbon in every color and design imaginable.

Hung on hooks were boxes of jewel-like Turkish Delight and chocolates to satisfy the taste buds of every chocolate addict.

A final touch had been an old but rich-looking Persian rug which added a touch of class and ambiance to the store.

Ava had managed to buy the entire stock of gifts and green houseplants from the gentleman who was relocating his family from Montreal to Toronto. For a bargain price, Ava had been able to purchase an array of shiny brass and copper plant containers, unique gifts and glass vases in every color of the rainbow. She was ecstatic with her stash, and he was elated to have unloaded his stock, in one fell swoop.

The doorbell barely stopped tinkling and satisfied customers left with arms overflowing with colorfully wrapped plants, flowers, trees and candy. They came and went exchanging a merry wink or a wave as they left the store. Customers mentioned that they thought the name "The Persian Garden" evoked thoughts of exotic beauty, and was very appropriate for this store. Many returned and became friends, lingering to admire the lush plants and flowers, mixed in with the glitter of brass, copper and crystal gift items.

Two weeks after The Persian Garden opened for business, Ava had to hire help to cope with the many admiring people that came into the store to look and then buy from the delightful selection of beautiful things around the store. The till was clinking open and shut every few minutes.

Jackie popped in after work at the hospital with her sunbeam of a smile and handed out the artfully iced gingerbread cookies that her mother and Ava made to the throngs of customers that came into the store. Ava was busy repeatedly reordering as demand kept increasing. At 9pm when the store closed its doors, Ava baked and iced cookies for the following day. Life had become a whirlwind of happy activity.

Every so often, her hand in the till would touch the "love letter" from Adil, that she had under the cash tray in the till and a bolt of anguish would shoot through her. However, keeping pace with business at the store and being exhausted when she finally got to bed, left her little time to think about Adil.
Jackie had noticed that Ava had not mentioned him in their recent conversations.

The first customer at The Persian Garden had been Madame Allard, who had swooshed into the store one morning, with a gust of cold wintry air. She looked winded from the climb up the hill and Ava brought out a canvas garden chair she had in the stock room at the back of the store for her to rest.

"Merci ma petit, je suis fatigue!" she said in heavily accented Quebecois French as she wearily lowered herself into the chair, resting her cane against the wall.

She was dressed in multiple layers of warm clothing, as if she was planning a visit to the North Pole. Heavy coat over several sweaters tightly buttoned around her ample frame, knee high Mukluk boots, hat pulled down low over her forehead and a voluminous scarf wrapped around her neck so that all one could see of her, were her twinkling blue eyes.

Ava shook hands with her as she chattered on in French, about the welcoming atmosphere of the store and beamed when customers entered the store and exclaimed "Mon Dieu, c'est un boutique vraiment beau!" and joined in agreement with a spirited "Oui, Oui!"

Madame Allard had become a repeat customer and looked around the store smiling and admiring the array of flowering plants, stooping to take in their fragrance.

Accepting a gingerbread cookie and a mug of hot chocolate, she leaned back, regaling Ava with stories of her family, and especially her much adored grandchildren.

Customers came and went. Unperturbed, she kept up her conversations with Ava and other customers as if they were all familiar. She watched Ava welcome clients, wrap their purchases in exquisite parcels of tissue paper, gift wrap or trendy burlap with lavish bows and a rainbow of curled ribbons.

If a customer was looking around indecisive about what they should purchase, Madame Allard made a suggestion and invariably the customer saw it her way and happily bought what she suggested.

"Remember, a fresh bouquet is uplifting and will always put a smile on your face," she said. "Flowers at work sparks your enthusiasm, mais oui! Flowers make the soul dance!" she said to customers.

After a few hours of relaxing, Madame Allard heaved herself off the chair with a loud sigh, complaining about the cold outside, her arthritic bones cracking, pulled on her coat, wrapped her long, thick, scarf around her neck and half her face, thanked Ava for the hot chocolate and took her leave, stepping cautiously on the icy pavement outside.

Ava sometimes wondered if Madame Allard had mistaken her store for a coffee shop, but she proved to be a dear soul and brought in all her relatives and friends as customers.

Three Christmas's had gone by in a flash as The Persian Garden continued to prosper as an enterprise.

Ava sighed contentedly, propping her feet up on an empty carton after she closed the door, on the last customer on Christmas eve.

Jackie had jumped up on the counter and surveyed the store.

"You did good kid!" she said biting into a gingerbread cookie.

Ava smiled warmly at her faithful friend, "Couldn't have done it without you pal!"

The store was sold out of almost everything except the large Balsam Fir in the corner, which Jackie was going to take home for her mother who celebrated Hogmanay rather than Christmas.

How do you feel about going home and having hot pizza and a glass of wine?" asked an exhausted Ava.

"Sounds like it would hit the spot perfectly, kid!"

"Okay, I am phoning in the order now so it will be ready for us when we get home... any special requests?"

"No, just the usual toppings for me!"

Switching the spotlight on an arrangement of tin soldiers in the window, Ava shut off the store lights and the two friends walked home in silent thought.

Chapter 37
A Change of Heart

It was a typical Durban evening, with a cool sea breeze gently blowing through the trees, from the tranquil turquoise sea on the horizon. The oranges and golds of sunset lit up the sky bathing everything in its rosy glow.

Ava's father put down his evening newspaper, his thoughts far away, one emotion after another crept onto his face like a slowly developing picture.

How many letters had he got from that darn fellow, Adil?

The letters had piled up over the last three years, collecting dust in the drawer where unpleasant correspondence go, to hopefully forever die. Pesky letters addressed in perfect cursive writing, that he wished would stop arriving, and free him from deciding what to do with them. He had wanted them to be discarded with the trash, but some invisible force held him back.

Instead of throwing them away he had surprised himself by instructing his secretary to file them under his confidential correspondence.

He had never replied to any of the letters, and had no intention of ever doing so, hoping that ignoring them, would result in stopping their arrival. He had considered sharing their unwanted existence, with his wife Dina, but thought it best she was kept in the dark about it, so as to avoid any discussion on the merits of replying to them.

Patience and consistency in ignoring them was the key to its demise, he figured. Receiving the first letter had made him angry. The impertinence of that man, to think he would entertain any part of his association with his princess of a daughter!

The weekly letters, came right on cue, every single week, for the past three years. He stubbornly refused to open and read any more than the first one, or redirect the ones, addressed to Ava.

He still begrudged the man, for spoiling his marriage plans for Ava, and now that she had a business instead of a husband, she would likely never heed his directive to marry a Parsee and settle down. He had not forgiven Ava, for going behind his back and meeting this Adil fellow, despite being forbidden to do so.

The only problem with this whole matter was that he loved and missed his Spanish princess Ava, and longed to hear her voice and peals of gleeful laughter.

He remembered how she loved to stomp around in the freshly cut grass, the numerous debates with him, where she fiercely held her own so admirably, and her baking that perfumed the home. He had obstinately refused to speak with her, despite his wife Dina nudging him every so often, to bury the hatchet and make contact. But now, with the frequency of his chest pains, he thought it may be time to make his peace with the daughter he so profoundly loved.

Dina, Ava's mother, sat across from him on the verandah, with her embroidery, occasionally glancing up at the garden.

"How lovely the zinnias and dahlias look today," she said.

"The watercolors of those sweet peas, their tendrils climbing up the fence!"

"Dina, when did you last speak to Ava?" her husband asked abruptly cutting through her thoughts.

Without looking in her direction, he could feel she was taken aback at his question, and staring at him dumbfounded. For three long years, he had refused to discuss anything to do with Ava, and maintained a resolute silence about her, and the events in Bombay that had caused their alienation.

"Darius, she phoned two weeks ago; don't you remember?" Dina said.

"Why would I remember? I did not speak with her, did I?" he said irritated that she would suggest he had forgotten anything.

"The next time she calls I need to speak with her," he said in a flat voice. Darius was a proud man, and it would not do to let Dina know that he might have softened his stance towards Ava.

"We could phone her right now, Darius," Ava's mother eagerly suggested.

"No need for that," Darius said, curtly putting an end to any hope Dina may have had, of an early reconciliation between them.

Over the years, Adil's letters remained the same, pleading with him for information of Ava's well-being. Every week, for three years, a letter had arrived at his office, asking for news of her, together with a letter addressed to Ava.

Darius had ignored his pleas, and scoffed at Adil's declarations of love for Ava. He had convinced himself, that the whole episode regarding Ava and Adil, had been an inconvenient family embarrassment and the matter was best left firmly in the past.

Lately though, those unwelcome weekly letters, now made him feel unsure of the stance, he had adopted for all those years. His mouth formed an expression of someone who had just tasted something distasteful. Clearly, he felt conscripted into a duty he found embarrassing and unpleasant.

Had he been wrong about this young man?

Nonsense.

He brushed the thought aside, as he smacked his newspaper firmly, trying to rearrange it. He found it impossible, to concentrate on reading any of its content.

After a wide-eyed night, spent tossing and turning and punching his pillow in an effort to get comfortable, Darius made a decision.

Taking the pile of letters addressed to Ava out of their "coffin" drawer, he stuffed them into two large envelopes, addressing them to Ava at The Persian Garden.
He attached a brief note that read: 'Ava, I am very proud of what you have achieved. I have your business card with me and see it every morning. I love you my dear daughter. After a moment, he signed it, "Daddy."

Next, he wrote a short note mentioning the address of The Persian Garden, placed it in a small envelope, and addressed it to the person that had sent him those weekly letters for the past three years.

Staring at the phone, tempted to call, he sighed, thoughtfully, his finger running along the edge of the red embossed business card of The Persian Garden. She had told her mother, that she was sending them her first business card and he had kept it proudly, gazing at it every morning before he began his day's business. But he had kept this information to himself.

He held his pride tightly to his chest. It was his armor against an everchanging world, he did not understand. It had prevented him, from speaking to Ava each time she called. But this was his little girl, the sun-kissed little one who bounced in his lap as a toddler, who made delicious crepes for the family, and grinned, watching him savor them.

After sixteen long years of illness, Ava had grown into a willowy, delicate beauty, with a caring disposition. It had never occurred to him, that she would ever oppose him. The shock of it had hurt him, and made him dig in his heels, in simmering indignation. But his love for Ava was now overtaking his resentment.

The realization that his actions might be wrong, was new and disconcerting.

The phone rang at The Persian Garden and Ava picked it up automatically answering with a "Bonjour, The Persian Garden!"
Darius cleared his throat several times and finally said, "Hello Ava?"
Ava cautiously asked… "Daddy?"
He had not heard her say "Daddy" in three years and his composure began to slip. He steeled himself, paused, and then continued, "Ava, I have mailed you some letters I received."

His tone made her resist asking who the letters were from. She guessed he was having a difficult time fighting his pride. The long silence between them, broken at last, was like manna from heaven and she hung on to his every word and nuance, enthralled and grateful.
"Daddy, how are you keeping" and then when there was no immediate reply, she said, "Mum mentioned you were having a problem with your heart; I really hope it is not serious."
"No, no nothing like that, I am fine," he said regaining his gruff tone.
"Ava, I do love you… look after yourself… I worry about you… you remind me of myself, when I was a young hot- headed rebel!"

Ava had been thinking about her dad and mum's own love story and wondered if she dared ask him about it… she hesitated…. there was a brief silence that seemed like an eternity.
"Dad, wait, I have something to ask you but you must promise not to get upset or angry with me," Ava said biting her lip as she waited for his response.
"Well, what is it?" he asked.
Since she did not detect any anger in his voice, she cautiously continued, "Dad do you remember writing to mum's father, asking for his permission to marry her?"
"Yes, what about it?" he asked, impatiently.

"Well, Dad, if you remember the response you got, was a definite "No."

She paused, and then taking a deep breath, continued "Dad, you did not accept his refusal to let you marry, because you loved her and only her, do you remember?"

There was a long silence and then he quietly said,
"Yes, yes, it was a very long time ago, but I remember."
Sensing she had come to the end of her dad's patience and not wanting to endanger their fragile peace, she ended their stilted conversation with the words, "Dad, I really love you."
His throat was constricted with emotion and for once he was speechless.
When he did not answer, she repeated. "Dad, I love you, goodbye for now."
"Goodbye Ava, I love you too. my Spanish princess." he replied in a hoarse voice and hung up, choking on long held back tears.

He shifted uncomfortably in his large office chair, thinking about the questions Ava had asked him. When he married Dina, he had been a poor student, and she came from a wealthy jeweler family. Darius rarely showed emotion, comfortable in his role as authoritative patriarch. Now, he felt remorse, billow within him.
Silent tears poured down his crumpled face, and dropped to be absorbed by the envelopes on his desk, that lay waiting to be mailed.

Chapter 38
Snowfall

Snowflakes danced like ballet dancers in the air.

Trees, houses, cars and people hurrying to their destinations, looked like icing sugar had been sifted over them.

Snow made the world look pristine clean, ready for new footprints, Ava thought, as she glanced out of her store window.

The snow drifts piled up along her large store window giving it the frosty look that allowed Ava to draw hearts on the glass.

She loved this time of the year. The scenery outside her store window looked like a picture postcard of a winter wonderland.

Children bundled up against the cold, their cheeks rosy, their scarf-wrapped faces smiling at being pulled along in a sleigh by their parents.

Lovers thinking about how they would make their partners feel special on the fast-approaching Valentine's Day. She knew flowers were the symbol of love, respect and admiration for most lovers. Love was definitely in the air as Ava scribbled down orders as fast as she could.

The Persian Garden phone had been ringing all day with Valentine's Day orders for flowers. She would have to triple her order of long stem roses, she thought, as she hastily drank her morning espresso coffee, and ate a croissant in three bites. Picking up her mobile, she phoned her supplier with an urgent request.

"Hello Pierre, I am going to need an additional thirty-six dozen long stem roses, mostly red, please."

The wholesaler she always dealt with for her cut flowers, hummed thoughtfully on the line.

"Ava, I can hardly get enough roses for myself," he said in a strong French accent. "But I will receive the fresh flowers from Amsterdam and we will share this order, yes?"

Ava thanked him, saying, "Bon, merci! Pierre, cherie, I have orders to fill and the way it's going I might need more than thirty- six dozen!"

"Ah well! I am happy for you!" he said enthusiastically.

"I will call Amsterdam, Holland, immediately and hope we can both get more roses... and I am guessing you will also need more baby's breath and ferns too, eh?"

"Oh, yes, yes please. Merci Pierre!"

"And what will I get in return, ma cherie? You know je t' adore!" he teased.

Pierre had a florist store on the other side of the city and was happy to place bulk flower orders for his store and The Persian Garden. Over the years, he had helped Ava with The Persian Garden, hoping that she would move beyond what he considered, her long lost love. She knew Pierre could not understand how she could be in love with someone she had not seen, or heard from in three years. She could picture Pierre shaking his head in disbelief, with his dark curly hair wobbling like springs.

Pierre sighed deeply, as he put a call through to his supplier in Amsterdam. Perhaps, this Valentine's Day would be different, and Ava would put her regrets aside, and realize it was futile to pin her happiness on an imaginary love. He would find a way to convince her this Valentine's Day, he promised himself.

The shrill ring of his phone interrupted his thoughts.

"Oui, oui," Pierre assured the Dutch supplier, "receiving the shipment the day before Valentine's Day is tight, but fine. Merci, mon ami, talk to you soon, eh."

He hung up, relieved at the good news. Ava would get all the additional roses she requested, plus the other flower varieties she had ordered, for her growing business.

Chapter 39
Valentine's Day

Ava saw the pearly light against her curtain, and slipped out of bed before dawn, on Valentine's Day. Showering and dressing quickly, she pulled on her boots, coat and scarf, turning up the fur-lined hood and walked the two blocks to her store.

The aroma of fresh-baked croissants wafted from the corner bakery, scenting the cold morning air. With a warm paper bag of hot chocolate croissants in her pocket and a fresh cappuccino in her gloved hand, she hurried to the store.

Letting herself into the quiet darkness, she took a few moments to think through the day's agenda as she shook of her snowy boots and unwrapped her scarf, slipping into a pair of pumps she kept under the counter. Sipping on a hot coffee and nibbling on the croissant, with her coat still on, she made a list of the things she had to do this morning, and later, when her shipment of flowers arrived. Pierre, her wholesaler, had promised to deliver them directly from the airport.

She gift-wrapped four dozen flowering plants, in silver and gold wrap printed with hearts, adorned them with a myriad of colorful ribbons and bows, and then slipped them into an extra cone of gift wrap to guard against the cold.

She stretched as she finished wrapping the last of the fuchsia-colored azaleas, which she noted with pleasure had dozens of buds ready to open into a glorious profusion of blooms. Quietly satisfied at the rows of multi-colored, gift-wrapped orders, each with their heart-shaped greeting cards stapled to the foil, she tidied up the store and waited for her cut flower order.

Dawn was breaking as she heard a knock on the door.
Through the glass, Pierre's delivery man waved to her. In came large boxes, piled to almost the ceiling of fresh cut elegant long stem roses, fine baby's breath, lush ferns, colorful alstroemerias, exotic birds of paradise and delicate orchids.

She opened each box with increasing excitement. She loved being surrounded by the beauty and fragrance of fresh flowers, damp greenery and lush ferns.

As she filled buckets of water to give the cut flowers a drink, before placing them in long gift boxes, she thought of the last three years. How quickly they had gone by and how she had grown both personally and in business. The Persian Garden and the people she had met because of it. The marvelous experiences she had enjoyed through the years had saved her sanity, directing her energy in a productive way. She had found a new life, and life had trusted her, to find it. The newfound independence and prosperity had given her the self-confidence she needed to dispel the dominance and disapproval of her father.

Inside her a sleeping giant awakened, forcing her life to take shape now, for love in her life. She realized that a life without love was no life at all, and she had to find it. Her longing for the comfort of Adil had not diminished with the passing years.

This was a part of her life that needed introspection. She promised herself to finalize this matter one way or the other, after Valentine's Day was complete.

While the roses had a long drink, Ava started to prepare the fifty plus boxes, she would need filled that day. Soon, she was up to her elbows in mounds of red and pink tissue, lining each long box and taping the correct greeting card and delivery address. As the day went by, the phone kept ringing with additional orders and she happily took each one with renewed vigor and pleasure.

Just before the midday sun shone high and bright, she completed filling all her orders and put the finishing touches to all the boxes, now piled ceiling high, in order of their delivery routes.

Jackie came in around 1pm and started to laugh.
"Oh my God! Look at all these boxes!"
"There's barely room to tip toe around. Ava, are you sure these are all your orders? We are going to need a large truck for these deliveries!"
"Geez, how are we going to get all this delivered today?"
Ava said, concerned, "Jackie, do as many as you can. Call up our pals and get them organized as well. Dear Pierre has offered to help if I absolutely cannot manage, but you know, I would rather not ask him for more favors."
The two friends looked at each other smiling nervously at the stack of boxes to be delivered.

"Jackie, are you free later tonight?" Ava asked in a serious tone.
"Sure kid, what's up?"
"Well…there's something I need to discuss with you. Shall we head up to our favorite café, and celebrate the day with some bubbly?"
"Hey! Sounds great… by the time this day ends we will really deserve the best champagne!" Jackie exclaimed, grinning.

Little by little, the pile of boxes and parcels disappeared into the delivery cars. The phone kept ringing, but Ava had to decline any further orders. Last minute customers, had come in, and bought absolutely everything she could possibly sell.

As the rosy gold sunset cast its shadows into the store, she gazed around realizing with pleasure that every vase, flowering plant and stems of cut flowers, had been sold. Her store was almost bare. Unbelievable, she thought, feeling tired, but elated. This Valentine's Day had broken all the previous sales records. It had been an overwhelmingly successful day.

The evening was turning into night as Ava got ready to go home, looking forward to a long bubble bath, and a brief nap, before meeting Jackie for champagne.

The store was still, as she turned on the spotlight, and put out the other lights. Looking back, she had a sense that something was amiss. Then she smiled as an idea took hold.

Placing a polished antique pedestal table in the center of the window, she draped it in folds of rich cream silk and scattered a few rose petals on it, from the dozen blush roses, she had kept for herself.

On top of the cream silk, she placed her grandmother's shining silver vase. Arranging it with long stemmed, regal, cream and pink blush roses, she stood back, to look at her creation. A stiff pink and rosy gold bow, added the flourish of elegance she was aiming for.

The spotlight in the window picked up the sheen of the vase, the richness of the cream silk, the glorious magnificence of the roses, giving the whole vision, an ethereal quality of exquisite beauty.

Wearily slipping into her coat and boots, she picked up her keys, and headed for the door. As she went out to view the window display, she realized that something was still missing.

What *was* it? She bit her lip, looking at her composition.

Why not leave it as it was?

Most people had gone home already, and few would go by her store, this late in the evening. Perhaps, she was being too critical, and simply needed that long-awaited hot bath and rest.

Firmly locking the store, she started up the hill to finally head for h me. She had taken the corner, when she paused.

For a moment, tears rose in her eyes, but she brushed them away and retraced her steps to The Persian Garden.

Going to the till, she picked up the cash tray, and reached for something unspeakably precious, below it. Taking it out carefully, she propped it up in front of the silver vase.

Now! she felt it was complete. Locking the door again, she looked at the window display from outside. It was everything she had wanted it to be.

Against the shining antique vase was a love letter on a leaf which read, "FOREVER" The promise Adil and she had made to each other.

The full moon was bright that night, as she walked up the steep hill, her boots leaving footprints in the snow. Later, bathed and rested, she answered the door to an exuberant Jackie. They hugged, relieved the day had gone better, than their wildest expectations. Now, on to celebrate their hard work, and bask in the comfort of their friendship.

After a few flutes of champagne, Ava thought the time was as right as any, to inform Jackie of what had taken place regarding The Persian Garden and other personal matters.

"Jackie, remember I mentioned I had something to discuss with you?"

Jackie, as always light-hearted and ready for a laugh said, "Yeah, sure kid, what's on your mind? Let me guess, a new business idea?"

Ava paused, then said solemnly, "Jackie, I have sold The Persian Garden. The deal was signed three days ago."

Incredulous, Jackie asked, "Ava why, why?"

Ava watched Jackie's face go through a gamut of emotions, like a pinball machine pinging.

Her mouth open, face flushed she gasped.

"What happened? not believing what she had just heard Ava say.

"Jackie, the challenge of growing The Persian Garden has been accomplished. It has given me more than I could have ever dreamed of, but... Adil is not with me, and there is an emptiness that even the success of my store cannot fill."

She went on, "Jackie, I have tried to reason with myself, to forget him, and perhaps, it is just a mirage, but I have to find out, and finalize this part of my life."

"Ava, you had not mentioned him in a while... I thought you were over him," Jackie said quietly.

"Adil is the man I love. I must find him, wherever he is," Ava said with conviction. She reached out and placed her hand warmly on Jackie's.

"I don't know what my next step is, right now, but I had to be free of The Persian Garden, before I made any plans."

"But are you not afraid of the unknown, Ava?

"You mean do I fear the future? Heck, Jackie after what I have experienced, I fear nothing. In fact, I look forward to life's challenges. The Persian Garden would never have been born, if I let fear get in the way! Remember, I have a toolbox of coping strategies, and I will choose *"Courage"* and *"Moving Forward"* as my tools, managing every challenge that comes my way, with finding solutions!" she said, feeling the fresh optimism, of opening a new chapter in her life.

She was quiet for a few moments and then said "Jackie, my volunteering at Médecins Sans Frontières has reinforced my gut feeling, that I belong in the medical field. I am cautiously... very cautiously optimistic, about finally studying to be a doctor. I now have the finances to pursue it. The Persian Garden sold for a hefty profit and I am no longer shackled to my parents' autocracy."

After a few moments of reflection, she said, "Jackie, did I ever mention Adil was ready to study medicine if my parents agreed to our marriage?"

"No! Really? He was prepared to do that?"

"Yes, he said he was, and then I stupidly fainted! Such a dumb time to faint!" she said reproachfully.

Jackie broke into a laugh, "Well kid, one thing is for sure, you are always going to surprise me!"

"Thank you, my dear friend... we will always be the best of friends, right?" Ava said, looking at her, affectionately.

"Sure, I would not miss being your best friend for anything!

Who else can shake me out of my shoes! You are a surprise a minute kid!" said Jackie laughing and crying.

They both got up and silently walked towards home, busy with their reflections, on Ava's bombshell announcements.

"Hey Jackie, do you feel like seeing the latest window display at the store?" Ava asked.

"Sure!" said Jackie, walking arm in arm with Ava.

As they approached the store, she noticed a small crowd of people gazing at the window. They had seen that before, and been amazed that someone would actually park their car, to look at the store window display. One by one, people returned to their cars. Only one man stood looking at the window, cupping his hands against the window as if he was trying to look deeper into the store.

Jackie caught Ava's arm.

"Ava, that man is behaving strangely, do you think he is looking to rob the place?" she said, concerned.

Darkness surrounded The Persian Garden, except for the glow of the spotlight, focused on the display in the window.

Jackie fished out her can of mace from her purse, and was ready to use it.

Ava could see the man's back. He had on a camel-colored wool coat, a brown Stetson, and was blowing on his hands, as if he was cold. She noticed he was not wearing gloves. He looks too well dressed to be a thief, thought Ava, but was alarmed at the intensity with which he was looking into the store window.

He turned.

Ava felt as if she could not breathe. She felt an urge to cry out, but instead found herself rooted to the spot.

She felt Jackie tugging at her arm, "Ava its freezing cold, come on let's go!"

She heard Jackie, but she could not move, staring at the man who had pressed his hands against the store window, looking inside.

The wind had picked up, and she could feel the cold bite into her gloved hands and Jackie's voice urging her to turn around and go home.

She suddenly broke away from Jackie, ran down the last few yards of the hill, stopping with her full reflection in the store window.

"Adil?"

The man turned so swiftly he almost fell on her. Their eyes met. He silently crumpled to his knees, his arms wrapped around her, his head buried in her coat. He was laughing and sobbing with profound joy.

"Ava, I love you, I love you," he whispered, over and over again.

Ava knelt too; her fear had turned to tears of unexpected joy.

There in the freezing cold, with snow falling like confetti on them, they embraced. Adil tenderly wiped away her tears and she caressed his away.

On their knees holding each other, shaking with incredulous happiness, Ava gave a shaky laugh, "Let's get up, Adil. I'm almost frozen into an ice statue! I'm sure you are too!"

He stood up, and without shifting his gaze from Ava's eyes, lifted her up and whirled her around and around, with joyous abandonment, oblivious of all else.

She saw Jackie over Adil's shoulder, stunned and transfixed by what she was seeing, shaking her head in disbelief and surprise, cheering with her fists up in the air.

The full moon was balancing on a rooftop, casting its golden splendor on the two lovers.

The love letters on leaves, they had written to each other, had found them. Their hearts overflowing with soul quenching love, they walked home, never taking their eyes off each other.

Ava was sure the angels sang, as the dancing moonbeams lit their way, together at last, forever.

THE END

Manufactured by Amazon.ca
Bolton, ON